THERE'S NO PLACE LIKE HOME

LAURIE CONDON

Black Rose Writing | Texas

The author grants the final approval for this literary material.

First printing

This is a work of fiction. Names, characters, businesses, places, events, and incidents are either the products of the author's imagination or used in a fictitious manner. Any resemblance to actual persons, living or dead, or actual events is purely coincidental.

ISBN: 978-1-68513-231-6
PUBLISHED BY BLACK ROSE WRITING
www.blackrosewriting.com

Printed in the United States of America
Suggested Retail Price (SRP) $20.95

There's No Place Like Home is printed in Minion Pro

*As a planet-friendly publisher, Black Rose Writing does its best to eliminate unnecessary waste to reduce paper usage and energy costs, while never compromising the reading experience. As a result, the final word count vs. page count may not meet common expectations.

Dedicated to Joan Russell
January 13, 1958- February 17, 2022

Although we knew you for only a short time,
your impact will last a lifetime.
May your memory live on forever.

If you enjoyed *There's No Place Like Home*, please check out Laurie Condon's first title, *Everything is a Big Deal, Until It's Not.*

THERE'S NO PLACE
LIKE HOME

PROLOGUE

Everyone has a story. My life was relatively uneventful until my husband and I hit a crossroads. We had a lapse in our relationship where we forgot to turn to each other. We had been together for all of our adult lives and had just started going through the "pots and pans" phase, as it is sometimes referred to.

It started in my late 40s. I guess I was having a midlife crisis and Gary, my husband, was dealing with his own situation.

There had never been a day that I hadn't woken up with an agenda of to-dos until one day I was lost and didn't know what to do.

In fact, for a brief period, Gary moved out.

During that time, I found myself surrounded by silence, which was truly deafening.

I missed all of the loud sounds that used to annoy me. How does someone make noise brushing their teeth?

This experience has taught me how fragile life is. We have to cherish every day and not take people for granted because time is fleeting.

I, Claire Holden, almost threw away my marriage. I am grateful I found my way back, but it very easily could have gone another way.

I will share my story in hopes of making you think very carefully about how you live your life and make your choices.

PART 1

Claire

I met Gary in college. I was studying marketing and he was studying accounting, so we technically could have met in a class but we met at a party instead. It's funny to think back to those days. I was reluctant to go out back then, always worried about being tired and eating and drinking too much. I wondered if other college students had those types of thoughts too or were merely just wondering whom they would go home with.

At any rate, he looked like he had walked right out of a J.Crew catalog, and I was interested. So, as usual, I put on my standing bitch face, which seemed to appear whenever I got nervous.

Thankfully, he didn't notice and approached me and we started to talk. We hadn't stopped for years, until we did.

For some reason, in my youth I always crushed on guys who were the opposite of what really appealed to my gut. The jocks who partied, broke rules, and misbehaved caught my attention. However, if they uttered a word to me, I would panic and get myself away as quickly as humanly possible.

Gary was similar in disposition to me, had no game and was a rule follower. While he wasn't "exciting" per se, from the moment I met him he felt like home. There was no anxiety around wondering if he was going to call. He was, and I was going to answer.

I realized how nice it felt to be myself and not pretend liking to do things. I had never paid attention to how many times a guy would say he was going to call and didn't or took charge of the plans without regard to my opinion. Gary cared about what I wanted to do, he was reliable, and he made me feel safe.

He was honest, easy to talk to and funny. He called when he said he would and planned. We fell into a rhythm, and I couldn't remember a time without him.

We were in our late 20s when he popped the question, and I couldn't have been more thrilled. We were on the same page in regard to a lot of major life decisions and, if we weren't, we were able to discuss things. So what went wrong?

I guess in hindsight we stopped communicating. Something I will never stop doing again.

Gary

I couldn't believe at 53 years old I was renting an apartment like I was back in college. I had a hot plate, mini fridge, a six-pack of beer and some ramen noodles. I was sleeping on a futon, and there was only one lamp.

My heart felt empty, but I didn't see a choice. If I were being truthful, I should have opened up to Claire like I had done since the day I met her. She was so easy to talk to and always came up with a solution. I remember a problem I had in my senior year of college when I needed a tax accounting course to graduate. There was only one time that fit into my schedule because I had a job in addition to a full course load. I had no idea what I was going to do. Next thing I knew, Claire went to see my teacher and somehow convinced him to let me in the class. Although embarrassing, it was quite effective. She always got price adjustments when things we bought went on sale two days after the fact, she got all finance charges waived, and when it came to our son, Drew, she would do anything to make sure he was treated fairly. Her productivity was unparalleled.

However, my problem couldn't be fixed and I hadn't wanted to burden her.

I knew in the end her heart would be broken one way or another, but perhaps I should have let her in. I almost didn't, until my half-sister gave me some life-changing advice. I will always be indebted to her.

I was adopted when I was 3 years old. I was actually born in Canada to a single mom who couldn't afford to keep me.

My adoptive parents didn't tell me much, and I didn't probe for fear of upsetting them so it was never discussed. They were older and super sensitive to any questions around my adoption. In fact, my adoptive mother told me no one wanted me because one of my ears was bigger than the other. I was constantly looking in the mirror to make sure they were even. I even asked Claire to measure them once. She humored me, but I am sure she questioned my sanity.

I knew that my biological mother was young and couldn't afford to keep me, but that was really it. That and my ears.

As I got older, I did start to wonder more about my biological parents, what they were like and all of the obvious questions you can imagine when you know you were given up.

As a parent, I found the thought of giving a child away unimaginable. Creating another human being was a miracle, and I used to stare at Drew in wonder. I remember examining his little toes and fingers and feeling a love that is hard to put into words. However, I wasn't alone when I became a parent, nor was I a teenager with no money. I'd like to think that I would have found another way than my biological parents did, but it's always easier to imagine what you would do if you were in a hypothetical situation. In reality, nine times out of 10 you would act entirely differently than you might imagine.

Not wanting to upset the applecart, I went on with life only thinking about my biological parents when I went for a medical exam. The doctor would ask about my history and I would have to say I had no idea.

One day on a whim, I decided to register with Ancestry.com to see if I could locate any information about my biological family. Not getting too invested, I swabbed my cheek, paid my money, and waited to see if anything would come of it.

Months after I sent the kit back, I got a note on the site from a guy named Arthur Murray. First off, try Googling that. There are only about a million dance studios and Arthur Murrays that come up. Arthur wrote a note saying that he had determined he was a cousin on my mother's side but wasn't very familiar with the details of my adoption. He told me the little he knew, but it was progress. Something I had never thought possible.

It felt strange to be having this dialogue, but there was a sense of belonging that I had never had before. I was tied to a family.

I was only able to glean a little bit of information about my mother. She was unwed and unable to care for me, but that was about it. She had died at a relatively young age, but I didn't find out much more than that.

I started to dig for more information and learned that all of the females in her family were unmarried and had kept their maiden names.

I knew nothing about my biological father, which was a big disappointment. But again, I wasn't expecting much and this was more than I had known before.

Claire

The wedding was magical, and I continued to pinch myself. I'd always imagined being married and having a family of my own one day, but I wasn't always sure it would happen. When Gary proposed I suggested we do a tiny cocktail hour. Then I went to a wedding vendor showcase, and I ended up booking a smoke machine, a live band, a chocolate fountain, the works. I felt like a princess.

Gary and I loved being married. Every year on our anniversary we opened a bottle of wine and watched our wedding video in its entirety. We relished every minute and often talked about how lucky we were to have found each other. We didn't fight and often found humor in the same things. We used to do so many fun things together, like the mud run we did two years in a row until I fell off the rock wall and decided a nice walk might be better. We went to museums, hiked, frequented bookstores, and then we just stopped. It seemed like there were more errands to run and chores to do around the house and we just stopped making plans to do fun things.

We truly enjoyed each other's company and would always rather be together than with anyone else. Perhaps we got complacent? Making time to go on those dates had made a difference.

In all honesty, I was always afraid that having a child would take away from our love, but it only intensified our connection.

Drew was born two years after we got married. He was perfect in every way, and we were truly living the American dream. The three of us were inseparable.

Although I loved being a mom, I found the days at home while on maternity leave to be endless. My best friend Lynn was pregnant, so we spent a ton of time together. She told me about her morning sickness, and I told her about my sleepless nights. But at the end of the day life was playing out in a wonderful way.

I always felt so lucky after spending an afternoon with Lynn because, unlike my marriage, hers was fraught with angst. Her husband was very jealous and wasn't excited about them having a baby.

While Gary went to every doctor's appointment with me, Jimmy, her husband, was absent from the majority of her checkups.

Gary cut Drew's umbilical cord, and Jimmy wasn't even in the room with Lynn.

I almost had trouble understanding how I had gotten so lucky. Not that I was waiting for the other shoe to drop, but I thought this was too good to be true. It wasn't, though. I was blessed.

I went back to work after three months, and I will admit it felt nice to be around adults. I loved Drew, but there was something really gratifying about completing tasks and receiving praise for a job well done.

When you are a parent, your job is never done and you never know if you are doing things right. In hindsight, there really is no right or wrong—there are merely good and bad choices.

I remember telling Gary shortly after Drew was born that I wanted to continue our date nights together. I didn't want us to lose our romance just because we were parents.

We got babysitters and made an effort to still have our own time too. We started hanging out with couples we met through Drew's daycare. As time went on, we found a few couples we liked to spend time with and others that we just phased out. I thought it was great that Drew was being entertained and we could socialize as well. It was a win-win. (In my eyes.)

Gary

I did love being a husband and a father, but between taking care of my aging parents and working, it was a lot to keep up with. Claire made tons of plans for us. Plans with people I had never heard of. That woman could make friends picking up dry cleaning. That was great for her, but I didn't need to fill every moment of every day. In her defense I didn't tell her how much it bothered me, but the weekends were filled with playdates, couple dates and errands. It was mentally and physically exhausting.

I think one of the things that drew me to Claire was her zest for life. I, however, just wanted to participate at will.

We didn't fight that often, but I finally had to say something because I felt like she was controlling everything. When we were going on four years of marriage and were exploring the idea of having another child, I opened my mouth and let her know that the constant running around wasn't making me happy.

At first, she seemed so deflated I felt like a monster. But I think after it set in, she started to contemplate that although we were similar in many ways, we also had many differences. Ultimately, we didn't have to be joined at the hip for everything.

After she got over the initial sting, she decided that she still had every intention of fitting in as much as she possibly could into each and every day. However, she was also going to give me an invite but carry on if I chose to stay home, which was my happy place.

This new arrangement was great for our relationship.

After discussing the chaos of adding another child to our family, we decided that we were going to stay a family of three—with the potential of getting a puppy at some point.

I thought I would have wanted more kids but I felt stretched pretty thin, and once again we found ourselves on the same page.

Claire

Gary had taken the wind out of my sails when he told me I was overbooking us. I guess I never really thought much about the fact that he might not like the double dates I had been scheduling. I think I was so afraid of losing myself when I became a mother that I had made a concerted effort to keep our social life thriving.

That's comical because having Drew only made us busier. We were now socializing with all of the new families we had met. If I were being honest, I was tired myself. Finding balance was very difficult, but I didn't want to miss out.

I was a little hurt by his words, but I also was relieved that he felt comfortable enough to tell me that I was making too many commitments. I tried to pull back a bit. I had to put his feelings before others and respect his wishes too.

I was also having some of my own struggles trying to keep up with my single childhood friends, my married friends, my friends through Drew, Gary's friends, and all of the parents. I felt guilty saying no to plans, but I hadn't really thought about whether I was even enjoying myself.

So, after mulling it over and lots of back and forth, I agreed to slow down and I also agreed that we couldn't handle another child.

I said I would consider a dog, but I kind of didn't mean it.

Gary

I was relieved when things finally started to slow down. It was like a burden had been lifted after I told Claire my true feelings. I kicked myself for waiting so long. It made me realize that no one was a mind reader. It was unfair of me to assume she would know that I was unhappy without saying anything. As soon as I did, I felt lighter. So why didn't I tell her about what I was going through?

Anyway, more on that later. We decided to put Drew into Tee-ball. Seemed like the right thing to do, and he loved it. Although we have a million adorable pictures, when you don't keep score and kids get as many tries as it takes to hit the ball, these were long days. Long, but fulfilling. I felt like I was giving my son what I had been denied by being adopted.

It made me wonder why my adoptive parents had become parents. They never seemed particularly engaged in anything I was doing. I didn't feel that overwhelming love from them that I had for Drew.

Sometimes when Claire wasn't looking, I caught her marveling at our boy and I was overcome with emotion.

I would never let him feel unsupported or unloved. I was more determined than ever to find out about my roots. I considered hiring a private detective to see if I could locate my biological father.

The more involved I became with Drew, the more I felt like something was missing. I wondered how my biological dad could forego the opportunity to take me to a ball game and miss out on this father-son pastime. Did he even know I existed? I had so many questions but no one to ask.

I continued to check my iPad and visited Ancestry multiple times a week. I heard from Arthur infrequently and he contacted me if he recalled anything. He told me more about his own life in Canada, but he didn't really know my mom. I needed to find out who my dad was.

Claire

Upon reflection, I might have been the cause of our demise. When Drew was young, I used to marvel at how other moms made juggling motherhood, work, marriage, and life look so easy. I was tired, resentful, and downright overwhelmed.

Lynn and I were very honest with each other. While she told me about her marriage issues, I told her about my feelings of being trapped and out of energy. Exhausted to my core.

"I think I may have just what you need," Lynn said.

"Two million dollars and a plane ticket?" I quipped.

"Have you ever heard of Beans, Black Beauties, Co-Pilots, Red Dexies, Study Buddies or Truck Drivers?"

I thought she had flipped her lid. "I don't know what you're talking about."

It turns out her friend Nicole had a son Drew's age who was now in ninth grade and struggling with paying attention.

He was driving her crazy and she took him to a doctor, who diagnosed him with ADHD. He started taking Adderall and soon became the best-behaved kid on the block.

Nicole had done a little research and decided to swipe a couple of his pills. All of a sudden, she was focused, energized, not very hungry and was losing weight.

Clearly there was a correlation, so she continued to investigate a way that she could get her own prescription, and suddenly there was a new hot topic amongst the PTA.

Their town had the most alert, focused, trim moms on Long Island.

Lynn slipped me two little orange pills, and my life was never the same.

Gary

Claire was acting like the Energizer Bunny. We were having five-course meals for dinner, the laundry was folded neatly, Drew was entertained, and she was surpassing her sales goals and doubling her commissions. She got extra money after she reached her quota. It sort of made me feel inadequate but happy at the same time. I loved not worrying about the expense of upgrading to the sports package on our streaming service.

She was truly amazing. I was in a good rhythm at my job as well, but sometimes my mind wandered off to thoughts about my biological dad. Ever since I had opened that Pandora's box it was hard not to think about where and who he was.

My adoptive parents fought all of the time. They never seemed happy, and I couldn't understand it. I imagined a whole different life. Not that there was much use in wondering about it, but it did nag at me.

At this point Drew was really getting into baseball, and I was taking him to games. Early on he asked me who he should root for. We lived in New York, and he was debating between the Mets and the Yankees. I told him the Yankees. I figured if he went for the Mets, he would be in for a whole lot of hurt.

I'm an idiot because now instead of driving to Queens where the Mets play, I had to drive to the Bronx for the Yankees. It was fun, though.

I had never played a sport at school, which I regretted. I think it's so smart to get children involved in sports, not only for their bodies but for learning to be part of a team. It's great for a child's social life, and especially good if you are shy. Drew seemed to take after me in that regard.

Claire

When I left Lynn's house with my two orange pills, I really hadn't planned on taking them. In general, I made a concerted effort to limit the number of any kind of pills I took, including Motrin, Advil and anti-biotics. However, these were taking her PTA by storm, and I was starting to feel like I was missing out.

I was scared about how they would affect me but also excited at the prospect. Maybe it would give me the jump in my step that I had been lacking lately? I had been missing that for a while and was looking for a boost.

I decided I would just take them once. I would take them when Gary and Drew were out of the house in case I started acting weird, but I would let Lynn know in the event I needed help.

If Nicole had given them to her son, how bad could it be for me a woman twice his size? I was assuming I might not even notice a difference. Drew stayed after school on Tuesdays, so that would be the day. Let the games begin.

Tuesday took forever to arrive. I got everyone out of the house, took the pills, and waited and waited. I didn't know exactly what I was waiting for. I tried to forget that I took them, but you can imagine how well that worked. I asked Lynn if she could get me a bunch so that I could be consistent for a good week. After I realized nothing crazy was happening, I started to analyze my every move. I noticed I could focus really well. I wondered if I actually had ADHD. This was miraculous.

An even bigger benefit was that my urge to snack and actually eat was almost nonexistent. I didn't know of any woman who wouldn't want to lose her appetite, especially after having a kid when losing weight was next to impossible. The only bummer was I wasn't sleeping that well. But I wasn't waking up tired, and I was firing on all cylinders.

I couldn't keep depleting Lynn's stock, so I needed to find my own supplier. I was afraid to mention it to my doctor, so I decided to join the PTA.

Gary

It was after midnight and I was watching my guilty pleasure, "Pawn Shop." Get your mind out of the gutter, it's "*pawn*." This is the show that people take the crap they have in their basement, get it appraised and make tons of money.

I was remembering the baseball my adoptive mother had gotten signed by every one of the original Brooklyn Dodgers and thinking about how rich we would have been if she hadn't left it in our previous house.

Pee Wee Reese, Don Drysdale, Sandy Koufax, probably Jackie Robinson too.

Anyway, no point in dwelling on that. It was that night as I was drifting off to sleep that I got a hit from Ancestry. This time it wasn't from Arthur, and my life was forever changed.

It was from a woman named Jean Kroscall who said she believed after looking at our shared DNA that we might be half-siblings.

My mind started racing, but it was really late and it wasn't registering.

I decided to write back to see if she had any further details. I almost wish I hadn't asked.

She believed we shared the same father.

Apparently, there were more of us. She had a sister, but my father had spread his seed far and wide and in total to date there were eight kids. Two wives, four baby mamas.

She proceeded to tell me that one of the many siblings was a historian named Henri (pronounced "On-ree") who had tracked her down and reached out about 15 years prior. Jean had a sister named Loretta. Loretta's husband thought it was a scam and encouraged Jean not to carry on the conversation. This was prior to the internet and Ancestry. When she finally got her own computer, she did a bit of digging on her own and reconnected with Henri. He had a lot of history to share.

It was after 2 a.m. and I felt a bit dazed and confused. I asked Jean if we could talk live the following morning. She was in Canada. She agreed and I went back to bed and tried to imagine how this story was going to unfold.

Claire

When Drew was born, I went a little off the deep end and decided he would have the very best of everything despite the cost.

He would go to Harvard but definitely first to Catholic school because that was his best route to success. As he got older and I learned that our public schools were really good and that St. Christopher's, down the block from us, catered to the rich, so I amended the plan. Although many students took advantage of the prestige, I had heard that there were others who got involved in drugs. There was a lot of money and many times money led to drugs. I was embarrassed to admit it but after considering our finances, I changed my mind and decided public school would be just fine.

Now I wondered if this could be the new distribution center for my potential lifeline.

How on earth would I orchestrate this? Tell Gary I wanted to investigate and pretend to be asking about the school for Drew? Would I pull a kid over in the hall and ask if he knew where I could score some Beans? For all I knew, only old people called them Beans. Should I say Study Buddies?

Ugh.

I had a habit of getting fixated on a thing and turning it into my thing. For example, when I was younger and was having trouble with math I hired a tutor and then I became a tutor and charged a higher rate than I was paying—so I actually got smarter and made money. Same thing for exercise. If I had to do it for myself, I figured, I would get certified to be a personal trainer and get paid for exercising.

Now if I was going to have to buy my Adderall, perhaps I could sell it. I sort of looked at this as community service for all my mom friends. We were doing everything, I mean everything. Our kids were in multiple sports, clubs, and extracurricular activities. We worked, we socialized, we were philanthropists, and we volunteered. I was just fueling my people.

Gary

I had no idea why I didn't talk with Jean the night she called because I counted every minute of every hour waiting until we could properly talk. I had so many questions. Of course, I didn't want to scare her away, but we had a lifetime of history to catch up on.

The next day I dialed her number, and the knot in my stomach twisted. After a few rings, Jean picked up the phone. I felt like I was calling a new girlfriend. My voice came out an octave higher, and I introduced myself. When it was her turn, she said she had been anticipating the call.

"I believe we have the same father," she said. "His name was John O'Brian. I have a sister named Loretta. We knew our father had a son who was adopted, and I am guessing that is you."

I couldn't speak for a minute. Finally, I squeaked out, "Wow, it looks like I have two half-sisters."

I asked her if our father was still alive. My heart raced. She let me know that he was deceased.

I felt a loss for something I had never had. I thanked her profusely for reaching out and asked if we could stay connected. All of the questions I wanted to ask had disappeared from my mind.

I hung up the phone and told Claire. She was equally dumbfounded. There had been no information for so long and this magical tool called Ancestry had revealed an entirely new history.

After I regained my composure, I sat down and wrote out some questions that I wanted to ask Jean. The most pressing was my medical history. I imagined maybe my biological father had high blood pressure, high cholesterol, eczema or some non-threatening condition. I wanted to know so that when I went to the doctor and he asked about my medical history I would have some answers, especially now that I was a parent myself.

I thought the best way for me to communicate with Jean at this point was via the computer. When I heard her voice over the phone my mind started to wander and I dreamt about a different path. Then I forgot everything I wanted to ask.

So I wrote back and thanked her so much for the call.

I then proceeded to write that although this might be awkward, could she provide me with any medical history I should be aware of? I also asked if she knew anything about the circumstances of my birth and adoption. I only knew that my mother was young, single, and unable to care for me. I was guessing this was the result of an affair.

I hated to ask, but I was sure she could sympathize about how unnerving it was not to know anything about your roots.

Claire

I gathered a bunch of Drew's report cards and awards from baseball, put them in a folder and headed over to St. Christopher's. I really had no intention of enrolling him, but I had to get the lay of the land.

Upon entering, it looked just like any other school. When the bell rang, I saw the first difference. The kids were all in uniforms, which elevated the atmosphere. I have to say, it was an improvement upon the belly shirts and drooping jeans I saw when I visited Drew's school.

It made the kids appear older and more sophisticated, but I knew that was just an illusion. They were all doing the same stupid things, at least that was what I hoped.

I headed to the main office and tried to see if I could find a cluster of shady-looking kids, but the uniforms made it tough.

I tried to see if there was a group of boys with longer hair. Did that even make sense? How the hell would I do this?

If I hadn't made an appointment and used my real name and number, I would have turned right around. I headed inside to meet with the headmaster, and that was when I saw my prospective dealer. He was sitting on a bench, waiting to be reprimanded after my meeting.

He looked sort of sloppy with his long hair and vacant eyes. I thought he was my guy.

I decided to try my best while I was waiting to engage him in conversation.

He couldn't have looked less enthusiastic, but I wasn't stopping. I started rambling on about how I was thinking about enrolling my son in the school.

I was trying to get him to reply in sentences rather than grunts. I asked him cautiously what he was doing in the office, and he said they had found something in his locker.

OMG, OMG, OMG, I was so excited that it might be drugs. Was that wrong?

The secretary apparently had been calling my name, and after the third time I heard it. Shoot, now I had to go in there and pretend I wanted to get Drew in when all I really wanted to do was talk to my new friend.

His name was Brian. I wished him good luck and tried to figure out a way to find him again after I got out of my meeting. It would look really weird if I asked him for his number. It would be worse if I tried to make a play date. After all, Drew was in ninth grade.

How *would* I do this?

Gary

I decided to write Jean a second note, with a disclaimer. If she felt uncomfortable sharing, I would understand. I would just feel better knowing if there was anything I should be aware of.

I sent the note and tried not to check my device every five minutes. I had been so distracted that I almost didn't notice that Claire was never home anymore and we hadn't had any plans for some time. I wasn't complaining, but I suggested going on a date. I had been daydreaming so much I felt like I didn't know what was going on in my own household. I couldn't believe I had two half-sisters. They were both a decent amount older than me. I wondered what type of relationship they had with our father. I couldn't believe I said "our father." Crazy.

Then Jean sent the following response.

Hi Gary, there is a medical condition you should know about. It is called Li –Fraumeni Syndrome and can lead to soft cell cancers. Specifically, brain, liver, lung, and sarcomas. You will need to have a genetic test to find out if you are a carrier. If you are, your children if you have any, should also be tested. The good thing is it doesn't skip generations. Meaning, if you don't have it neither will your children.

Unfortunately, I have it, but Loretta does not. I am currently on my third bout of cancer, so that sucks. All I can tell you about our father is that he left us when I was 7 and Loretta was 4. We didn't see him or have any contact with him until I was 20. That only happened because his father died, and we went to the funeral. He had two more daughters in his second marriage. They both died of cancer. He also had another daughter in France, who died of cancer and a son, Henri, who is still living in France. I was born in 1958 and Loretta was born in 1961 and I am assuming you were born after us. Are you married? Do you have children and where do you live?

Thanks for getting in touch and I hope we can keep in touch if you would like.

My head was spinning.

I felt paralyzed but knew I needed to reach out to my doctor immediately. I decided not to tell Claire until I had a game plan. I didn't want her feeling the anxiety I had.

I left an urgent message with the doctor's office and watched every minute go by until he called back.

Claire

I sat down with the headmaster and he started telling me about the legacy of the school, the statistics of who went on to college, and other facts about why I should enroll Drew. I have to say it did sound impressive—until he got to the tuition. It was roughly $10,000 a year. I could barely stomach that we eventually would be paying that for college, but high school? Not happening.

We certainly weren't poor, but we didn't have an extra 40 grand sitting around when Drew could continue in public school where his friends went and where he was getting a perfectly fine education.

I had almost forgotten the purpose of my visit as I listened to him. I started nodding my head in agreement and proceeded to barrage him with questions that made me look engaged while I thought about how I was going to track down Brian.

After the meeting concluded, I passed Brian heading in for his punishment, and I quickly asked him if we could continue our conversation about my son when he got out.

He sort of rolled his eyes. "Whatever," was his short response.

I walked outside into the hallway and waited, trying to come up with a way to find out if he had what I needed.

About 20 minutes went by and Brian walked out. I asked him if he wanted to grab a coffee.

He looked at me like I had two heads. "I'm in ninth grade, I don't drink coffee."

"Right, right. How about a burger?"

He liked that idea so we drove to Five Guys. I'm sure I should have been concerned about someone seeing him get into my car, but I was distracted by how this conversation was going to go and, honestly, I didn't think anyone was really paying attention.

We ordered, him a burger and fries, me a Diet Coke, but, man, I really wanted those fries. But I digress.

He started eating and I began asking him how he liked the school and if he had many friends, etc.

Again, the vacant look.

I decided to cut to the chase.

"Look, I don't really care if you like the school, I was wondering if you could score me some Beans."

Again, a quizzical look. I sort of shouted, "You know, Beans!"

Silence.

"Adderall, Brian, I am looking for Adderall."

"Oh, why didn't you just say so? I can do that, but it's going to cost you."

Gary

The doctor called back and said, "That's amazing, let me get this straight. You found your biological family on Ancestry and now you could have a life-threatening disease? Sounds like a Lifetime movie!"

He sounded almost excited, which was disturbing. However, he reiterated what I already knew—that I needed to go for testing stat.

He gave me the numbers of a few genetic counselors, whom I proceeded to call in no particular order. The first couldn't get me in for three months. I hung up abruptly and tried the next one. It was only a four-week wait, but I didn't think I could take it. I tried the third, and this time I sounded frantic and told the woman on the phone that I couldn't wait much longer and was freaking out. She was empathetic, and she got it. She was able to squeeze me in for an appointment two days later.

I decided to go alone because I didn't want to panic Claire if this turned out to be nothing. That was mistake No. 1. If she were the one undergoing the test, I would have been furious and hurt if she didn't tell me. I wasn't thinking straight, and I really thought I was protecting her.

The next two days went by in a blur. When I finally was face to face with the doctor, he told me a little bit about the curse.

I already disliked my father.

Here's a recap of what he said.

Li-Fraumeni Syndrome is a disorder that causes an individual's risk of developing certain types of cancers to be significantly greater than the general population. Specific mutations an affected individual inherits from their parents are implicated in the development of Li-Fraumeni Syndrome.

I missed some of the gene mumbo jumbo, but the bottom line was I could be missing the tumor suppressor gene.

Here's more of what he told me.

The average chance of a Li-Fraumeni Syndrome patient to develop any form of cancer is 90 percent for women and 70 percent for men.

Around half of all cancers that develop in these patients are diagnosed before the third decade of life. There is no cure, and there are no symptoms.

Thanks Dad, you big asshole.

The doctor told me to swab my cheek—something I wish I hadn't done on Ancestry a few weeks back when I had no idea about any of this—and the results would take about three weeks.

How on earth was I going to act like nothing was on my mind? This was a potential death sentence, but why worry Drew and Claire when I might not have it?

So I took the test and started waiting to find out about my fate.

After I got home, I reached out to Jean on Facebook chat. I barely knew her, but she must have understood what I was feeling since she was living through my biggest nightmare. Since I hadn't told Claire, I was really alone with my thoughts.

Jean was very compassionate. She suggested that I reach out to Henri. That actually excited me and distracted me for the time being, and I decided to do just that.

Claire

While I knew I was at Brian's disposal, I was still the experienced adult in this scenario.

I figured before he tried to extort me, I would drop some statistics on him. I let him know there were a lot more of me (once I got involved in the PTA) and he could either take advantage of me or strategize with me to drum up some real business from my mom network.

Those vacant eyes started to twinkle, and he let me talk.

I had to think on my feet because I hadn't even been to a PTA meeting yet, but perhaps if I showed the women how much I was accomplishing they would marvel at my energy and efficiency.

That was my plan, so I proceeded to explain to Brian that I thought after the moms saw what I could get done, I would steal the floor and offer them my "vitamins."

Brian saw the potential, and I decided to pay for the first batch—thinking this could likely be more lucrative than my career.

Again, I had to remember not to lose focus on the real goal here, which was to feel better. Having a plan of action and a solution to my sourcing issue empowered me, and I felt fantastic.

I was in such a good mood that I decided to offer Gary and Drew takeout and a game night. Gary had been distracted, which had worked to my advantage, but it also made me suspicious. He kept running upstairs to message someone on his iPad. He said it was his half-sister, but I wasn't sure if I was buying it.

Drew had been holed up in the basement with his headset on, screaming with his friends around some video game. I felt a little guilty about not limiting his time on those mind-numbing devices, but I was plotting my logistics. His grades were fine, and he was a lovely kid, but this was really substituting for my lack of parenting. Useful, but I still felt guilty.

I drove home from St. Christopher's and called up Drew's school to find out how to get myself entrenched in the PTA.

In general, a pretty clique-ish bunch, but I thought when they saw that I wanted to participate in *everything*, I would get a warm reception.

Gary

I decided to friend Henri on Facebook, which was a good thing because he only spoke French. The chat translated the messages, otherwise we wouldn't have been able to communicate.

I typed and erased, typed and erased, and finally led with, "Hi Henri, Jean tells me you might be my half-brother."

I saw the three dots, indicating he was responding.

"Yes, I am the French brother. So hello to you and your family from France."

I felt elated. He sounded so warm.

He proceeded to tell me that he had been on Ancestry for 15 years, trying to research his history. I didn't even know it existed that far back.

He next told me that there was a law in France called "Delivery Under X." That meant if you were adopted, you couldn't get any information about your origin.

He then wrote something that was so sentimental.

"To be adopted is no easy way to live, we need maybe more than anybody kindness and love. For we are injured inside."

I agreed wholeheartedly. No one really understood what it felt like, and he had just summed up what I was feeling. A tear ran down my cheek.

Henri was able to tell me that our biological father had passed away in 1994. He was living with a wife, which was neither my mother nor his.

He had two daughters with her. The first was born in 1972 and died from brain cancer. The second was born in 1976 and died from bone cancer.

The first was 30 when she died, and the second was only 19.

My mood shifted immediately. This was a result of the Li-Fraumeni Syndrome.

Suddenly I was exhausted. It was actually after midnight for Henri, so I asked if we could continue our conversation in the morning. He replied that he was so happy to be in touch, and I powered down my iPad and tried to get some sleep.

Claire

I never in my wildest dreams thought I would be going to a PTA meeting, but at 7:30 p.m. that's where I was headed.

Everything I did would determine the success of my new venture. I had been so preoccupied with this plan lately I could barely focus on getting through all of the other tasks on my daily agenda. Which were plentiful.

Normally, I tried to make sure we all ate dinner together, but I hadn't been enforcing it because I was too busy plotting. What would make these women want to be like me?

I even bought an outfit to make sure I looked cool and confident without overdoing it. I didn't want to look like I was trying too hard, just sure of myself, and comfortable in my skin.

I wore a nice outfit from Sundance Catalog, which always got me compliments. I sat down and assessed the crowd. I felt like I was a student again, trying to hang with the popular kids. Meanwhile, up until this very moment I had concluded that the PTA was a group of women who never fit in at high school getting their second chance.

Not once had I considered this was just a group of moms trying to make sure their kids had every possibility available to them.

Anyway, I digress.

I cased the joint and saw about 20 women I needed to impress, befriend, appeal to their busy schedules, and try to offer them energy in a little pill. Maybe not at the first encounter, but I needed to set the stage.

I was thrilled to be given the floor to introduce myself. I laid it on a little thick, but they ate it up.

"Hi ladies, my name is Claire Holden, and my son Drew is a ninth- soon to be 10th-grader, and I just want to make sure that he has every amenity under the sun at his disposal so that he is primed for success. He loves sports, and of course I want to keep the equipment well stocked and help raise money for the school so that they want for nothing. What can I sign up for?"

Their smiles lit up the room, and they fought among each other to get me on their committees. I had no clue how I was going to fit all this in. Perhaps I would use a few weeks' vacation to focus on the PTA.

There went our summer trip, but it was for the greater good.

Gary

I of course had trouble sleeping but couldn't quite seem to get motivated to get out of bed. I couldn't believe it had only been three days since I had sent the test in.

I decided to reach out to Henri again and learn some more about my history. He proceeded to expand upon what he had told me the night before. In France you are forbidden to investigate adoptions. They are all closed, and the records are sealed.

Henri decided to ignore the law, feeling that it was his right to know, and I didn't disagree with him.

He had a knowledge of law and historical research and had a friend in the state administration office who allowed him to get access to some records in order to investigate Loretta and Jean a bit further. When he began his research there was no internet or social media, so it was a tedious process done through mail.

Loretta's husband thought the letters he sent were a scam, so Henri didn't hear from her or Jean for quite some time. Jean also was suffering through her first bout of breast cancer, so they didn't connect for many years.

I asked Henri if he knew what our father had died from. He had to try and find the English name for it. Oh yes, prostate cancer. Universally a horrible disease.

He asked if I wanted to know anything else about him. I said I would love to know everything about him. What did he do for a living?

Henri said he enlisted in the Air Force in Canada where he was a mechanic on planes. At one point in 1958 he was stationed in France whereupon he met Henri's mother. He told her he was single, but he was actually married to Jean and Loretta's mother.

So, clearly, she got pregnant. He promised to marry her, but he supposedly had to wait on some paperwork from Canada. She had the baby, who was Henri's sister. They continued their relationship, and she was pregnant again (with Henri) and then a priest from the military base told her that our father was married and had a daughter and another one on the way with his wife.

He gave Henri's mother some money and went back to Canada.

Henri said his biological mother's family was ashamed and angry, so they said they would keep the girl but give him up. They actually said they didn't want the boy. His mother fought for him, but it was rough times and she didn't have financial support, so she gave him up.

He was eventually adopted by a family, but it took months because he came down with a mysterious illness. During that time our father left Jean and Loretta's mother and probably met my mother. He quit the Air Force and decided to become a truck driver.

Henri said he had collected hundreds of pages of information and spoke in depth with Jean and Loretta and a cousin with a good memory to obtain all of these facts. He also got our father's military files and his divorce papers. Our father had a sister named Amy, who died of bone cancer. Her daughter was the cousin Henri connected with.

Next Henri very casually asked me if Jean had told me about the murder.

"What?" I screamed. "There's a murder?"

He said I needed to take a seat for this one. Our father had a brother named Kieran who, by the way, died of liver cancer. Kieran was an alcoholic. Really a violent nasty guy. Our father hated violence or any conflict. Clearly, he was a lover, not a fighter—as evidenced by his eight children. Or at least the eight that we knew of.

Anyway, Kieran was drunk one night. Their father, Grampy, was also drunk. Annihilated. They started fighting and Kieran pushed Grampy down the stairs. Grampy fell into in a coma and died a few days later.

Kieran landed himself in jail. Henri said despite all of the stories he couldn't help but think our dad was just seeking love. With each woman there was new promise. From all accounts he was charming with a soft voice. Henri thought that in his last marriage he was faithful, but that was tragic too since both of his daughters died of cancer. Just a sad story all around.

My God. My head was spinning. I thanked Henri profusely, and he seemed equally grateful to have someone to discuss this with. I wished I had told Claire so I could tell her about the murder, my many siblings and Henri, but I still needed to know if I had the gene.

I decided to wait.

Claire

I was so invigorated by my new project—my mood was markedly improved and everyone was noticing. Gary and I actually planned a date for Saturday night. It had been ages since we had gone out, in fact. I couldn't really remember the last time we connected in both ways, mentally and physically.

I still think he is one of the most handsome men I have ever laid my eyes on and that, coupled with his personality, made him perfect. But if I was being honest, I didn't have the same urges that I used to. I don't think it was at all based on him but more on my age and my schedule. I used to want to jump him whenever I saw him. Now I want to cuddle on the couch and eat popcorn. He is still my guy, but, man, no one really talks about aging until it's too late and you're in it. I was hoping my new "vitamins" would return me to the vixen I once was.

Since I had started taking Adderall, I felt so much better. I started to panic about not being able to access it. My arrangement with Brian was working out fine, but what if he moved? Or flunked out of St. Christopher's? I was scared to have all my eggs in one basket.

I did a little research and learned that Adderall was highly addictive, but I was so sick of worrying about something being good or bad for me. I needed help now, and right now this was the way.

According to WebMD, Adderall was a stimulant. A combination of amphetamine and dextroamphetamine that was commonly used to treat ADHD, a hyperactivity disorder. I remembered when Minoxidil was used to treat high blood pressure and then it was discovered that it helped with hair loss. Or Gabapentin, which was used to treat nerve pain but also prevented seizures. Maybe I would prove that Adderall, initially used to treat ADHD, had a host of other bigger benefits such as weight loss and energy for middle-aged women.

Apparently, the medication worked by increasing dopamine, the feel-good hormone, and norepinephrine levels in the central nervous system—the brain. Who'd want to come down from that?

The one thing I had noticed was that I had to adjust the dosage. As time went on it took a little more each time to get me to the same happy place. I wasn't concerned, just paying attention. I would never go this route but supposedly it worked faster if you snorted it or injected it. I would have felt like I had a problem if I started doing that, which I clearly didn't. In fact, I had never been more on point. I was killing it at work, I was running three committees of my own on the PTA, and I was damn popular. I had about five women who had joined me in the vitamin game, but slowly the buzz was picking up. It was just a matter of time until I got the entire group on board.

The only downside I saw so far was that I was a bit anxious and I wasn't sleeping—but I wasn't tired.

Gary, who wasn't the most observant, paid me a compliment as I headed out the door one night. He asked me if I had lost some weight. I had never been heavy, but my new loss of appetite was having a positive effect.

I also thought Drew felt proud when he saw me interacting with other moms at school. I had always tried to go to his classroom and read when he was younger, watch him in school plays and attend his baseball games. But as he got older, there were fewer opportunities. This just elevated my engagement without cramping his style.

Drew

Something weird was going on at my house. My dad was constantly on his iPad. He had stopped nagging me to toss around the ball with him. My mom, who usually scrutinized my homework, hadn't asked me if I had even done it. Normally I wasn't allowed to play video games during the week, but I had been in the basement playing games and eating snacks every night for the past few weeks. Apparently, the no-food rule in the basement had been relaxed.

We hadn't eaten dinner together as a family in forever, and all of our food had been takeout.

I tried to eavesdrop on their conversations, but all I heard were conversations about the PTA from my mom, which was bizarre since she always had made fun of these women in the past. My dad was chatting with someone named Jean, but it didn't seem like anything interesting.

All the changes were to my benefit, but I sort of missed the old dynamic. Being nagged made me feel loved in an annoying way.

I didn't really feel like I could talk to my friends on the baseball team about how I missed family dinners. What teenager would complain about getting takeout every night?

My parents used to watch TV together and now they were both going off and doing their own thing. Maybe they had a lot of work, but I liked knowing they were watching their nerdy shows together.

They used to finish each other's sentences. Now they were barely talking. I hoped things would go back to normal. I grabbed some Doritos and decided if it kept up, I would ask my mom if everything was OK.

This new routine was making me anxious.

Claire

I couldn't believe I was nervous, but Gary and I hadn't been out on a date in forever and I wanted to make a concerted effort. I felt I had been neglectful and distracted—it wasn't on purpose, I just had a lot on my mind. He seemed a bit preoccupied too, but I hadn't asked him what was going on because I kind of didn't want to know.

I would make sure I gave him my undivided attention. Up until this point, I had only taken my Beans during the week, but I thought I would take some before the date to make sure my energy level was up in case we decided to have sex.

We set Drew up on a "meet-up." I was tempted to tell him it was a "play date," but that might have gotten me shot. He was too young to stay alone and too old to have a babysitter. Gary and I headed to our favorite restaurant, the one where we had celebrated numerous anniversaries, birthdays, and other momentous occasions.

I wore a dress, totally unlike my normal boho tops and jeans. Gary had on a button-down and khakis. He looked really handsome.

We ordered a nice bottle of wine, which we usually didn't do because of the expense, but decided to splurge. We weren't cheap, but we were in the practical phase of our marriage. I had made the dumb declaration once about how flowers were a waste of money, which they are, but a surprise once in a while would have been nice.

Anyway, we toasted to reconnecting and catching up.

I started by apologizing for being so distracted and told him I had joined the PTA and that it was like a full-time job.

Gary was clearly stunned.

"I thought you hated the PTA and thought they were a group of women who never found fame in high school looking for a do-over."

"That was me just being judgmental. I owe it to Drew to be more engaged."

He seemed impressed with my new endeavor and asked me to tell him about it.

I felt guilty because the lies came so easily.

I told him about the bookfair and the car wash and how we were getting new lacrosse equipment for the school. I described some of my new "friends" and told him I had actually gone to a pocketbook party with them.

Mind you, I didn't need another bag. In fact, I was a bit of a bag snob and would never buy a knock-off, but going to these parties was how I was going to find new customers. The parties were the perfect forum for me to tell the women about my laser focus and how I had dropped two pants sizes without being on the Peloton for months. My Lululemon outfits were strictly for walking the mall.

I asked him about what was keeping him entertained these days. He casually told me he thought he had connected with more of his family through Ancestry, but nothing too interesting.

He brought me up to speed on Drew's new love for pitching and how he planned on taking him to the batting cages. I was suddenly relieved. As preoccupied as I had been, it was clear that we could always just go back to our easy dialogue and fall right back into step.

Gary asked me about my new energy, and I told him I was taking a new protein powder. He also mentioned that I looked very fit. I said it curbed my appetite, so I had dropped a few pounds.

We finished off the bottle of wine, and I felt good and a bit amorous. Thank God. I hadn't had an urge in so long I was starting to worry.

I looked at Gary. "Want to go back to my place or yours?"

He chuckled and we hurried home.

We had the house to ourselves, and we kissed. It was really nice and we proceeded to go up the bedroom because as cool as it looks in the movies, having sex on the kitchen floor, dining room table or standing up is truly just not as comfortable as the good ol' bed.

So it had been a minute, and I was sort of nervous. Things seem to close up down there if they haven't seen any action.

We started fooling around and one thing led to another. Although I was consumed by lust for Gary, it was taking me a long time to climax, which was making me anxious, which was preventing, you know ... So I did what I had never done before. I faked it. I now had a new worry. What the hell was going on?

Gary went to clean up and I grabbed my phone and asked Siri, "Does Adderall prevent orgasms?"

Siri immediately replied in her robotic voice.

While alleviating impulsivity, hyperactivity and depression might sound good, these effects can also lead to a lack of sexual desire in women. In fact, women might even find it very difficult to achieve orgasm, and they may also experience lubrication issues.

Are you fucking kidding me? I was shocked. I had fixed one problem and created another. Since my acting skills were on point and Gary was none the wiser, I wouldn't have to figure this out immediately. But I was freaked out.

Gary

Claire had looked really hot recently. With all of this new information about my potential health issue and my intense conversations with Henri, I hadn't had a minute to figure out if she had bought a new gym membership or changed her diet. Whatever she was doing, it was working.

We were headed to our favorite restaurant to see if we could connect and catch up.

I had been feeling like I was just going through the motions in order to get to the meeting with the genetic counselor. I couldn't understand with all of the latest advances in science why I'd have to wait three weeks to get the results. I wasn't even through the first week yet. It felt like it was taking forever, and I was having a hard time concentrating on anything else.

This restaurant was special for us. It was where we celebrated every life event and occasion of significance.

As usual our conversation picked up right where we left off, and things felt normal. I realized how much I had missed this. I needed to try and stay more present. Claire filled me in on what was happening at work and how she had joined the PTA. I was shocked to learn that. She had always insisted that they were a bunch of snobs. I was impressed that she had put her love for Drew above her dislike for this group of women.

She seemed a little jumpy, but I attributed it to her new endeavors. It seemed reasonable to be jittery with all of the new responsibilities she had taken on. So I really didn't think much of it. In hindsight, I wish that I had.

After dinner, love was in the air. Come to think of it, we hadn't had a bottle of wine in some time, and it got us both in the mood.

I felt like a schoolboy. It was really good to reconnect with Claire on all levels, if you know what I mean. I was proud of her managing to fit in the PTA with her busy schedule. I think she was concerned about losing Drew's affection since he was in the weird teenage rebellion phase.

He was certainly no trouble, just a lot of grunting, dirty socks, video games and constant hunger.

I would call that totally typical.

He now preferred to hang out in the basement. I remembered a time where we couldn't get rid of him. You know, "Can we play a game? Do you want to watch 'Kickin' It? Can we go to the park? Can you take me to McDonald's?"

It was just another phase of life gone by. Suddenly I panicked, thinking about if I had the gene, what if I had given it to Drew?

If I understood correctly, if I have it, there is a 50/50 chance he might have it as well. If he has it, he will need to be screened every three months for the rest of his life.

I hated my father for several reasons, but this was the biggest of all. I tried to push those thoughts away since I still had another two weeks to wait.

Was it better not to know? I didn't think so. I was really surprised that Jean, who was going through her third bout of cancer, didn't have her kids tested. They were old enough, I guess, to decide on their own, but collectively they had decided not to pursue it.

I could understand if there was nothing you could do if you found out. But although there was no cure, you could absolutely treat the cancer—no matter which kind—if you caught it early enough.

I don't know why I didn't confide in Claire when we were on our date. She was going to be furious. It was just that Claire had so much on her plate, and she didn't have a ton of patience. I was hoping that when I told her, it would be after I found out that I didn't have it.

The last time I spoke with Henri I had asked him if he had gotten tested. Again, he was the same age as Loretta since my dad had impregnated his mother and her mother at the same time.

He hadn't gotten tested. We talked about it, and he said he was too petrified. I think that after all of our conversations, he was considering getting tested too. Especially because he had a daughter, who of course would have to be concerned if he had the gene.

He told me that because the health-care system in France is socialized medicine, you could end up waiting months for your results. I had been waiting a mere seven days, and I felt like I was going to crawl out of my skin.

I decided to reach out to Jean again and ask her if she had included her husband from the beginning. She had been battling this for close to five years, in remission and then not one but two recurrences. I wondered if it had affected their marriage.

I did know, from what I had read, that women have a 90 percent chance of inheriting the gene, while men have a 70 percent chance. Still crappy odds, but there was a chance I wouldn't have it.

I decided to go for a run, something I hadn't done since the fifth grade. I didn't even know if I had sneakers, but I needed to do something with this nervous energy.

Claire had been lecturing me about my sedentary lifestyle for years, and this was the impetus it took to get me moving.

I found some sneakers and told Claire I was going for a run. She literally almost fell off her chair.

I told her I was listening to her advice and knew I was getting long in the tooth so I was going to start moving.

She looked very perplexed, but I put on my AirPods and went. I made it down the block and could barely breathe. OK, so I would make this a walk/run, with the goal of completely running as I built up my stamina.

Claire

I nearly fell off my chair. Gary just told me he was going for a run. I thought to myself he just needed to get laid more often. That's on me. I was proud of him. He was behind a desk the majority of the day.

Imagine if I gave him an Adderall. He would want to do the marathon.

Speaking of Adderall, I was so upset about the sexual side effects. Maybe I was overthinking it and maybe it was a coincidence, but I had noticed that it was a little dry down south. It didn't help that I was nearing 50. I had heard 50 was supposed to be the new 40. If my eyesight and crow's feet were any indications, this was in fact a lie.

Maybe I would call the gynecologist and just ask, for a friend of course, if this could be a side effect of the Adderall. I wondered if there were something to counter it.

I couldn't imagine not having this newfound vim and vigor. When I thought back to life before Adderall, it made me depressed. However, sex is really important in a relationship. I would need to figure this out.

Anyway, there was no sense worrying about it now. I had to head over to the school for the junior prom committee meeting, and it was delivery day. I now had eight moms placing regular orders, and a few others suffering from FOMO.

I had worked out a great deal with Brian, so I got my supply for free and turned a profit.

I suggested he get a new pair of jeans that didn't hang down to his knees, but he wasn't interested in my fashion advice.

I started to breathe a little and actually relish in my new side hustle. It was picking up a nice rhythm, and no one was the wiser.

Everyone was a winner. Moms were happy. Check. Kid was happy. Check. Claire was happy. Check. Gary was happy. Check. But he wouldn't be if I didn't get my mojo back. I was a fixer. I would fix this.

Gary

I returned from my walk/run and I realized that I was an old man. Holy shit, I was so out of shape. I decided I was going to do this daily. I'd been setting a horrible example for Drew, sitting on the couch watching TV. I thought that next I should look up foods that fight cancer.

I started Googling around, and the first common thread was no processed or packaged foods. It seemed like the idea was to avoid foods with toxins, chemicals, or antibiotics.

Pretty much my entire diet. I shouldn't say that. Claire subscribed to one of those meal kits where they send you the ingredients and recipes and, supposedly, everything they provided was organic. I was guilty of grabbing lunch from 7-11 on occasion, and I did love me some Swedish Fish, but seemed like sugar was a no-no as well.

Leafy greens seemed to be a cornerstone in all of the recommendations I found. I couldn't hate kale more, but I did like salad so that would be easy.

I learned cruciferous veggies were also great in the fight against cancer. Ooh, cauliflower! I wondered if cauliflower pizza counted. There was also broccoli, cabbage, and organic meats.

Apparently, organic meats had detox properties that could balance your hormones, not to mention they could eliminate viral infections and fight cancers.

Lastly, it looked like I needed some herbs. Turmeric, raw garlic, basil, oregano, thyme, cayenne pepper, parsley, ginger. I decided to head into work late and ran over to Whole Foods.

I came back with an array of kefir, kombucha, seeds, nuts, and a bunch of other weird things that I could honestly say I had never heard of. I grabbed a pamphlet near the door that had a few recipes.

Next, I decided to go to Best Buy and grab a blender.

Are you aware of how many different types of blenders there are? Daunting. I got talked into a Vitamix, which sounded very healthy but set me back hundreds.

Could you put a price on health? I instead decided to take the whole day off from work and started making some smoothies to see what I could concoct.

I destroyed the kitchen but came up with a few really good blends. I brought a glass over to Claire. She was very diet conscious so she gladly accepted—with skepticism.

"What has gotten into you? Do you have a new girlfriend?"

I laughed it off and said of course not, I was just taking her advice.

She went back to her phone call and raised a glass (of green juice) to me.

I felt better already. If I had the Li-Fraumeni Syndrome, I was going to fight like hell to keep it at bay.

Claire

I decided that I was going to proposition Gary to see if the other night was just a fluke. Hopefully I would be able to climax if we tried again and I could stop worrying. It was almost like trying to get pregnant again, scheduling a session. I needed to know that my inability to "O" was an anomaly.

I was afraid my thoughts would get the better of me, so I decided I would have a glass of wine with dinner to loosen up my lady parts.

Gary had been acting really weird lately. I had been nagging him for nearly two decades to start exercising more. He was trim, but it was what was going on inside that I was concerned about. I joked and asked him if he had a new girlfriend, but in the recesses of my mind I wondered if this were a possibility.

He actually went running, which was bizarre. I was thrilled, but I was sure I made a face because I was so astounded.

Then he made me a smoothie. That was even more startling. He couldn't even cook cereal, so to whip up a smoothie that tasted somewhat decent was no small feat.

Maybe he had started reading the AARP mailer that talked about it never being too soon to start taking care of yourself.

I called the gynecologist's office and made an appointment. As usual unless you were in labor, the office was booked three months out. I was offered an appointment with her physician's assistant, which actually might be better. I didn't think I wanted my doctor to know I was taking Adderall. I doubted it would get back to her if I met with the PA. I took the appointment for the following week, which gave me relief just knowing I had it. Let's see if I could relax enough to get the juices flowing on my own.

Gary

I cleaned up the kitchen after making enough smoothies to last the week, and I asked Claire if she wanted me to start dinner.

"What the fuck, Gary?"

"Woah, just a simple question."

"Running, I think good. Juicing, you are finally coming to your senses. Cooking, midlife crisis. Now I am worried that you have a tumor or something. What is going on?"

"Can't a guy just try to help his lovely wife out?"

"No, you are acting really weird, and it's freaking me out."

In all honesty, I had just wanted to add a shit ton of herbs and cruciferous veggies to the meal. Rather than explaining myself, I said, "You had your chance, but don't say I never offered."

I guessed I would go reach out to Henri.

Henri responded almost immediately. I started by saying, "How is it going, bro?"

"Aw, bro, I am good, how about you?"

We continued and I asked if he had any pictures of our dad and he sent some over. He was a really handsome dude, which didn't surprise me since he had bedded quite a few women and it also explained my good looks.

It made me sad.

I looked to see if there was any resemblance, but I couldn't really tell. It reminded me of when someone has a baby and people immediately say, "Oh, he looks just like you." To me, babies all look pretty much the same. I never notice any resemblance until they are at least 2 or 3 years old.

Henri continued.

"Years before I began to search about my origins, I was a history and geography teacher."

The more I learned, the more I was impressed with Henri. He seemed to be so well educated and worldly. He also had one of the warmest dispositions I had ever encountered.

He told me his DNA showed that he was 51 percent Scottish. He also told me that when he was a teacher, he used to organize an annual trip to England, Ireland, Wales, Cornwall and Scotland.

On one of the last trips, in Scotland, in front of all of his students, he told me he suddenly broke down in tears. "Deep within me, I was finally home. I didn't want to leave," he said.

A tear rolled down my cheek, thinking of all that I had missed.

I learned he was a big traveler. On the contrary, I hadn't left the country.

Speaking of resemblance, Henri and I definitely looked like brothers. It was the nose.

I asked him if he had been to New York since he was the big sojourner, and he told me he hadn't. I imagined our meeting up, although there was one obvious issue. He didn't speak English, and I didn't speak French.

Our conversation continued for close to another hour, and I learned that we had similar tastes in old movies, music, "Star Trek" and "Star Wars." That was no coincidence.

Speaking to him brought me a peace I had never felt before.

Claire

I sat in the waiting room, anticipating what would be discussed when I was finally called in for my appointment with the PA. I wondered if I should just come right out and tell her about the Adderall, or let her examine me first? Since I didn't know her, I decided to just come right out with it and hope there was a simple remedy.

The PA, whose name was Patricia, asked me what seemed to be the trouble. I told her that I had recently been put on Adderall (by myself, but I left that part out) and was noticing that sex wasn't as satisfying as it used to be.

I felt so awkward telling a stranger about my sexual issues, but I was sure she had heard worse.

"You are 50, right?"

Thanks, Captain Obvious, you are staring at my chart.

"Yes, I turned 50 two months ago."

"Let me put it to you as delicately as I possibly can. When you are young, your vagina is like shag carpet, as you age it is more like linoleum. Couple that with a drug like Adderall, you are going to have some issues."

My mouth was agape, and I couldn't speak.

Not the answer I was hoping for.

I regained my composure and managed to squeak out a question. "Is there anything I can do?"

She talked about hormone replacement, creams, lubes, and all solutions I hated to consider. I asked if giving up the Adderall would make a difference.

She said it might help, but Dyspareunia is a real thing that is a result of decreased estrogen levels. The vaginal tissues tend to become less elastic and more fragile, which can make having sex painful or even impossible. Add a drug like Adderall, which is known to cause vaginal dryness, and you are going to have intimacy challenges. However, it was more than likely that given my age I would still have run into some problems with or without the Adderall.

I told her I really didn't want to take hormones, which were linked to cancer. The thought of cancer was too scary to imagine, but now I was at a loss. I was desperate to save this sacred part of our marriage. I had lost three friends to cancer in their early 50s. After witnessing them suffer, there was nothing worth increasing the risk.

I knew if I talked to Gary, we could find other ways to stay connected. I was sure I wasn't the first woman to have this challenge, but I didn't like the alternatives that were being offered.

Again, I had always enjoyed sex, but it wasn't as important to me as the connection I felt it created. That was what I didn't want to lose.

Gary and I had been in lockstep for our entire relationship and suddenly I felt as if I should be put out to pasture.

I had a lot to contemplate. I thanked the PA and let her know I would be in touch if I wanted to discuss estrogen cream, but I knew I wouldn't.

I felt depressed.

I wondered if any of the PTA moms had had a similar experience. I didn't want to bring it up for fear of diminishing my sales. I suddenly felt alone.

I decided to go back online and see what foods could help with vaginal dryness. Here's what I found:

Cranberries
Sweet potatoes
Probiotic rich foods
Omega 3 fatty acids
Apples
Soy
Avocados
Dark leafy greens

These were the exact ingredients in Gary's last smoothie. Maybe that's why he had made it for me?

He noticed? Do I ask him? This was probably why he had bought all of those random ingredients. I felt so self-conscious.

Gary

Women! Claire freaked out about me making smoothies, and now she was sucking them down like they were going out of style.

Whatever the reason, I wasn't going to complain. I needed her to start using these cancer-fighting ingredients in our regular menu. I was a week and a half away from getting the results. It was getting more bearable because I had running and eating healthy on my mind, which distracted me.

I did have a serious talk with Jean, and she suggested I reconsider letting Claire in. I appreciated her advice, but I was so close to the results now I wasn't going to change course this far in.

Perhaps once I got the news, my opinion would change.

Her husband had been along for the ride, and in her case being there for the ups and downs of thinking the cancer was behind her only to have it come back. Jean said he had really helped her cope with the obstacles put in her path.

Hopefully this would turn out to be a scare I could put behind me.

While the reason I had started on this heathier journey sucked, I was happy that I was adjusting my diet and exercise now. I truly felt better. I was waking up with energy and starting to see a two-pack. I was nowhere near a six-pack, but it had only been a short time.

Maybe I could start Drew on this healthy path at a young age. It would help him with his baseball efforts, and it was something we could do together. It might be too late since he wasn't entirely excited to hang out with his old man, but I hoped he would indulge me.

I wanted to ask Jean why her children had decided not to get tested. I understood the fear factor, it was real, but still there were things you could do proactively. Once it was too late, it would be too late.

It wasn't my business to butt in, but God forbid if I ended up in the same boat there was no question Drew would be tested immediately.

I already felt guilty, which made no sense, since there wasn't anything I could have done to prevent my genetic makeup.

I wondered if my father knew that he had spread this gene. I was going to ask Henri when we connected again if our dad knew he had it. I was guessing he didn't. In fact, I had never heard of this syndrome before. The odds of having this gene were one in 20,000. This wasn't the lottery I wanted to win.

Thanks Pops, you son of a bitch.

Claire

I decided to go to CVS and casually peruse the lube aisle. Damn, I definitely wasn't the only one suffering. There were a million and one choices. I wondered why I had had no clue. I guessed it was like when you were, say, buying a new garage door, you'd look at every door in the area to get ideas. Or if you were putting in a new driveway, you'd notice details you had ignored passing hundreds of driveways.

I picked a few products and threw them into my cart. I felt like a teenager buying condoms so I picked up some other random crap I didn't need to camouflage them.

Of course, who do I see but Ginger from the PTA? She might have been the bitchiest member I had encountered. When I had asked her if she was interested in some "energy vitamins," she had dismissed me instantly. She said she didn't need any more energy.

She eyed my cart and smirked. She probably needed lubes too. I waved and looked away.

Of course, when I got to the checkout counter the lube was missing a price. So my charming cashier grabbed the intercom and said, "I need a price on Uberlube. I repeat, can I get a price on Uberlube?"

Fifty shades of crimson.

With the three smoothies a day and this stuff, I was sure I could fix what was going on with my body. At this point, I didn't feel like I could consider giving up my pills. They were my savior. I literally took them as soon as I got up and perhaps a booster in the afternoon if I felt like I was coming down at all.

I had never been more on my game. I was less distracted, more productive, engaged—in fact, I thought I felt awesome. I was moving so fast I couldn't even tell.

I was a bit jumpy lately, and when we were watching TV (which rarely happened these days) if something I didn't foresee happened, I screamed at the top of my lungs. Sometimes when I was deep in thought and the doorbell rang, I jumped out of my skin. I also found myself rambling. I almost couldn't stop talking. I hadn't really been making plans like I used to because I was so focused on my side business, my job and Drew that those date nights just hadn't been a priority.

I was also forgetting things. I would have a thought and lose it midsentence.

Despite all of these new side effects, I still couldn't imagine not having my little helpers.

I just wished there weren't sexual side effects and, coupled with my age, it was frustrating. Anyway, I was putting that out of my mind for the time being.

I had ideas of how I could remedy that on my own, and I was concentrating on expanding my distribution beyond the PTA.

I imagined doing my side hustle full time and not always having to run. It was a tricky balancing act, working full time and then selling Adderall on the side. If I could give up my job, maybe Gary and I could take up a couple's hobby.

I could potentially try running like Gary, although I didn't have fond memories of it. Gary seemed different lately. We were sort of like two ships passing in the night. Don't get me wrong, our date night was good— aside from the faking incident. I had also put effort into being more demonstrative and seductive, but I was preoccupied and I didn't feel very authentic. I didn't think Gary could tell, but now with him making smoothies, I was starting to wonder if he was on to me.

I didn't really know what to do, maybe I needed therapy? I also realized that I hadn't spoken to Lynn in weeks. We never used to go more than a few days. Maybe I would reach out to her and set up some girl time. I had been alone with my thoughts for too long and needed an objective opinion. I wanted to share my Gary concerns and see if she could give me advice in the bedroom department. I decided to call her and get something on the calendar for the following week. My mood was already elevated in anticipation.

Lynn and I finally met up at our favorite restaurant. It served all of our favorite salads. One of the many things that I loved about Lynn was her obsession with food. She was as nutty as I was, ate the same odd things I did, and really loved them just as enthusiastically.

I apologized to her for being out of touch, and of course it was as if no time had gone by. She said she had wondered why she hadn't heard from me, and I decided to fill her in on my PTA endeavors and, even more importantly, my new venture with Brian.

She turned white as a ghost and said, "Oh my God, this is all of my fault."

I proceeded to tell her that I was eternally grateful. I no longer felt so desperate. I was the goddamn Energizer Bunny.

I was also contributing to the PTA which, believe it or not, I felt really good about. She still looked horrified. I assured her that it wasn't an issue.

I explained it was really just like taking a vitamin. She looked skeptical, but I proceeded to tell her how it was helping me and she calmed down.

I confided a little more, which was a relief. I told her that I hadn't been able to climax since starting on the Adderall. Lynn and I shared everything from constipation to sex, so I needed to get this out. She asked if I had talked to my doctor, and I told her about the shag carpet to linoleum example. We laughed and cried.

She confided in me that she wouldn't know. She and Jimmy hadn't been intimate in months. I asked her about it, and she said not only was she too tired, but she didn't even like him anymore.

I thought of Gary. I still loved him. I had to figure out how to get back to feeling more connected. We continued on, and I asked her if she was considering getting a divorce. She actually said she was too tired to get divorced.

"What about those little orange pills you shared with me?" I asked her. "Why aren't you taking advantage? You would definitely have more energy."

She said she was afraid of getting addicted. I asked her if she took a multivitamin. I asked her if she took cholesterol meds (which I knew she did). She nodded. I asked her why this was any different, and I told her I would give her my rate. She seemed hesitant but hopeful, and in my persuasive way I convinced her to give it another try.

I couldn't love a person more than I loved Lynn. This was coming from a genuinely good place, but it would also be nice for us to share the experience.

I gave her some on the house to take home and see if she felt a little more energized. In regard to the sex advice, she didn't really have any since she wasn't having any.

I felt better by going out with a girlfriend. We made a pact to not let so much time go by, and she placed an order so we had a legit reason to meet up in a couple of weeks.

Gary

I decided to reach out to Henri again since I felt so much better after messaging with him. We literally could message for hours. Time went so quickly when we were connecting.

We exchanged greetings, and we started delving into our movie collections. I had hundreds and hundreds of movies. It turns out he did too. Many of them similar. Was that genetic?

Claire hated old movies, and Henri loved them. I was excited to talk about the old actors we both cherished. Then we talked about our favorite Netflix series and learned that we had several of those in common too. "Breaking Bad," "The Kominsky Method" and then we delved further into "Star Trek"—and I knew we were blood brothers.

He told me of some other shows that I would check out when Claire went to bed.

I realized I didn't really have a friend aside from Claire that I talked to. Of course I did when I was in high school and college, but after marriage and having Drew, I just sort of lost touch.

It was nice to have a brother/friend to talk with about guy things. I realized how much I kept inside.

He reminded me of the time difference and that it was after midnight in France. I apologized and thanked him so much for the time.

"Live long and prosper," he wrote.

I laughed and felt it in my heart.

I had a friend.

There was so much that I had never shared. My childhood was less than ideal. I had had the belt used on me. I wouldn't say I was abused consistently. However, I was ignored and hadn't experienced much affection. There was no hugging in my house. I felt more like a tenant than a family member. I realized after getting involved with Claire just what the potential could be. Seeing the interaction between her and her parents reminded me of "Leave it to Beaver." I couldn't believe it was real, but it was.

Suddenly, I longed for that. We had that type of rapport, and Drew only enhanced it. A guy needed friends, though. I didn't realize how I had longed for a confidante in addition to Claire. Perhaps to talk about

Claire with and question my feelings. Henri was going to fill a void I didn't even know I had. The healing had truly begun.

Claire

As I sat on the floor and struggled to mix the precise combination of paint colors to get the exact blue for the pep rally float, I realized that I had been blending colors for hours.

I was late, shit. I was supposed to be on an internal call with my boss 30 minutes earlier, but I couldn't get the color I had been envisioning and I was slightly obsessed. In my head, I realized no one was going to care what shade of blue I developed, but it seemed so critical to my float that I couldn't stop working on it.

I didn't even get to shower, but I guessed my team knew that normally I cleaned up well, so I scrubbed the paint off my hands, put my hair in a bun, and tried to pull myself together. I headed into the office, thinking I would say I had to drive Drew to school at the last minute and had totally forgotten about the meeting. I was sure it was no big deal.

I went to my drive-thru Starbucks and got a Trenta, which was like four cups of coffee in one. I'd already had my pills so now I was firing on all cylinders.

I rushed in, said my usual good mornings, and tried to slip into my office. I hadn't even been in there for five minutes when my assistant told me I was wanted in my manager's office in 15 minutes.

I was sure it was just for a recap, which was what we did in our weekly meeting, so I chugged down some more of my coffee and tried to switch gears. Maybe I could pick up some purple paint on the way home so I could get that blue to where I needed it to be.

I pulled out the project that needed my attention the most and tried to get my facts together for my meeting.

It was 9:30, and I walked down the hall into my boss Jeff's office. He asked me to take a seat. I apologized for missing our call and told him about the ride I had to give Drew.

He stopped me midsentence and said, "Is everything OK at home?"

"Yes, why would you ask?"

"You seem really jittery and on edge lately. I'm not the only one who has noticed so I just wanted to check."

Wounded, I said I appreciated the concern, but I just had a little detour and was on point.

"You have some paint on your shirt. Clean yourself up, you look a little disheveled. I think you should be closing that deal with Easton today, right?"

I confirmed that that was the plan.

"Claire, if you need to talk, I expect you to come to my office at any time. We've known each other for two decades now. I consider you family, not just an employee."

I thanked him and slinked back to my office. Wondering how I had gotten so sloppy.

In so many ways I felt laser-sharp, but I could see some of what Jeff was talking about. I hadn't been paying as much attention to work as I used to, and I could make more of an effort to not wear paint-stained attire.

I was hyper-focused on whatever I had started doing lately and had lost the ability to multitask. I thought a solution might be to calendar my projects so that I stayed on track. I guess because I had been at my job so long, I was letting the business run itself, which wasn't good. I truly owed it to the clients to put effort into their campaigns.

I called my contact at Easton and asked if I could take him out for a working lunch so we could check in.

He was pleasantly surprised.

We picked a location that allowed me to stop home and put on a clean blouse. We met up and had a nice lunch. I took copious notes and assured him that his project was moving along smoothly. The Easton campaign was delivering and now I had a great meeting to report back to Jeff.

I made it through the day, stopped at the paint store on my way home and continued furiously to blend colors until I got the perfect blue for a float for a bunch of 16-year-olds. For a hot minute, I saw that this was a bit irrational.

I'd been averaging five hours of sleep a night, but I wasn't tired, just jumpy. In the recesses of my mind, I knew that I was no longer thriving but rather surviving. I was worried that if I stopped taking the pills, I would gain back the weight back I had lost.

I was getting multiple compliments about my weight loss. I thought back on the many hours wasted running in place, sweating for hours to look exactly the same. Now I did nothing aside from walk around the block a few times and I was thinner than ever.

I would miss the number of things I could accomplish in a day. I was working full time, was on multiple committees on the PTA, had a flourishing "vitamin" business that was expanding, and I thought I was doing a decent job keeping up with the chores.

The only things that might have been suffering were our family dinners and perhaps our social lives. Honestly, Gary was happier staying home, and I didn't really miss it. I thought this was a victory. The one thing that had me on alert was he seemed to be going upstairs and chatting on Facebook with "Jean," his long-lost half-sister, a lot. I was going to ask about it. I was sure it was innocent, but he was definitely spending too much time holed up in our room.

Gary

The day had finally arrived. I was finally about to get the results from the genetic testing.

I was hoping that I would be able to go home and recap all of this for Claire, apologize for not including her, and promise to never keep anything from her again.

I sat down and so did the genetic counselor. He started telling me about how there may be a co-payment that wasn't covered and asking me HIPAA questions, and I blurted out, "Get to it, doctor. Do I have it?"

His forehead crinkled, and I saw a look of concern in his eyes. That was when I knew the answer. I had been sure in my heart I wasn't a carrier.

"Unfortunately, your TP53 gene has a mutation. This does mean you will have an increased risk of developing soft tissue cancers such as breast cancer, brain tumors, adrenocortical carcinoma, leukemia, and others such as prostate cancer."

I remembered that was what my dad had died from.

I wanted to cry but no tears came out. He quickly assured me that there were risk management options to detect cancer early or lower the risk of developing it.

Stunned doesn't even begin to explain what I was feeling. He continued on with dos and don'ts, but I missed a lot of what he was saying.

"You should avoid exposure to radiation," he said. "You should have a comprehensive physical exam and a rapid whole-body MRI, colonoscopy and once we see that you are clear you should plan to go for a checkup to Mount Sinai Medical Center every three months."

It sounded like a death sentence, but he assured me if I kept up with my screenings I could still live a full life.

He then asked me if I had children, and my heart sank.

I had to have Drew tested. I felt paralyzed.

Not only that, but the conversation I had to have with Claire was much different than what I had been imagining.

He asked me if I had anyone I would like to call or if I would like him to arrange an Uber so that I didn't have to drive.

I told him that wasn't necessary, and I walked back to my car in a daze.

I was desperate to talk to Jean.

Drew

My parents were acting really weird lately. My mom never even asked me about my homework anymore. I was doing it, but she used to make me go over it with her every night after dinner. I hadn't brushed my teeth in a week, but I was going to. That was actually just disgusting, and I felt a little guilty about it.

She hadn't even yelled at me for bringing food up to my room.

I wasn't really complaining, but she wasn't really paying attention to me. Same with my dad. He used to always want to go outside and "throw the ball around." I usually would rather play video games, but he assured me that I would look back on these times and be glad that I chose to spend time with him. I didn't think he was right, and I really wanted to play "Madden" on the PlayStation instead, but I usually went because I didn't want to hurt his feelings. Lately he hadn't even asked me, which was odd, but at least I didn't have to let him down.

I thought about asking to make sure everything was all right, but I didn't want to have my mom start reviewing my homework or giving up my video time so I decided not to say anything.

PART 2

Claire

I went to meet Lynn at her house with her first delivery to get her on board, and I wondered if I had forgotten my birthday. Gary was there, two moms from the PTA, Jeff, Lynn and another guy I didn't recognize, I am guessing my host? Holy shit, was this an intervention? I literally thought steam was coming out of my ears.

Why on earth would Lynn do this to me? I felt such anger. I looked at her, and she seemed as if she were about to burst into tears.

The stranger in the group was a therapist, who made an introduction and told me that my friends and family had sought him out because they were concerned for me.

They each went around in a circle, recapping specific behaviors about how I was losing control. This went on for close to an hour.

They explained what they saw as the problem, told me what they thought I could and should do, suggested I go to *rehab*, already enrolled me (against my will) and assured me that my job, my kid and my husband would be waiting for me upon completion.

I started to bawl. I was sure that I had it all together. What the hell was I doing that was so disturbing that resulted in an intervention?

As the stories went on, I learned that I was simply manic. I rambled, I produced way too much work, I was almost robotic, I didn't socialize anymore, I was jittery, and I was focused but somewhat distracted, if that even made sense.

If I stopped to think about it, it was true. I was up to four pills a day, and I actually had Googled how to inject it so that it would take less time to kick in. Somehow, although I proclaimed I would never consider doing that, I rationalized that I was just trying to be more efficient.

I had lost interest in anything that didn't support the PTA or my business and had stopped enforcing the few rules I had going at home.

Thank God Drew was a responsible kid who didn't require much assistance. Shame on me, though, he was my kid and he was acting more like a parent than I was.

I was never going to admit it, but I was sort of relieved that for the next 60 days I could stop running on this hamster wheel.

I was, however, a bit panicked since I knew that this was the end of my lucrative side hustle. I had really become reliant on that money. I hoped I could reach Brian before they carted me away to rehab.

Gary pulled me aside and told me that he was so sorry he had missed all of the signs. He said when I got back, we would have to have a talk but assured me he wasn't leaving. There was just something that he wanted to share about why he had been distracted. He felt terrible, almost pained. He started crying, and I crumbled into his arms and told him I was sorry and was going to get a handle on this.

In my heart, his words confirmed my greatest fear. I was pretty convinced he had been having an affair. Was Jean really his "sister?" I had been so distracted that if he had turned to another woman for affection would he really have been to blame?

How could I have ignored my marriage?

Jeff told me not to worry about my business, the accounts that I had managed for years would still be mine and they would be waiting for me when I returned.

All of a sudden, I screamed who will make Drew's lunch, what about the float? Gary reminded me that I never made Drew's lunch.

Janet from the PTA said she would take care of the float and that I had achieved the prettiest blue she had ever seen.

Lynn came over and looked like she was afraid to talk to me. She told me she hoped I wasn't mad but I just seemed to be a little … unhinged.

Wow, don't hold back, I thought. Unhinged, huh?

That was fair, and I was grateful that she cared enough to arrange this and risk my wrath. I asked her if she thought I was going to end up in a padded room. I was scared. I felt so out of control just leaving for 60 days. What would l I do without my Adderall? I started to sweat and shake.

She assured me that she had done her research and this was the best program around. I wanted to thank her, but it was too soon and I was still angry at her betrayal. So I nodded and walked away.

That was when Doctor Andy came over. For real? Doctor Andy? I already thought this wasn't going to work, but I shut my mouth and let him talk.

"Claire, this happens to a lot of people, and you can be helped if you are open to it. Do you want to get help?"

I couldn't honestly say that I did so I didn't answer, I just listened.

He told me about the program. Of course it was in Utah. Why couldn't it be in New York City? I guess I would be too close to my crutches if I did this as an outpatient.

After a really tough hour, maybe even more, we all left. Gary and I were in separate cars since I didn't know he was coming.

I think part of him thought I would take off. I succumbed. We both headed home, and I started to pack for rehab.

I knew I had a problem. I felt ashamed and embarrassed but I had to let Drew know what was going on.

He was a pretty smart kid, so he didn't look at all surprised, and just said, "You've always been there for me, mom, now let me be here for you."

I must have done something right. He was so fantastic and I burst into tears.

Doctor Andy met me at the airport and actually took me to Utah. Was I a flight risk? How much was this costing? I felt guilty and questioned the necessity. He assured me that it was covered and that I needed to focus only on my recovery.

The program was 60 days and was a lot of therapy, groups, art, groups, meals, groups, movies, groups.

I hadn't talked so much about myself ever.

I was now trying to think back to make sure I was never molested, abused, bullied, etc. Nope, I was just a middle-aged lost addict.

I learned that people who take large doses of Adderall for prolonged periods of time could and usually do become physically dependent on the drug.

So according to one of the counselors, my body had to "recalibrate" itself. The symptoms of the detox were my worst nightmare:

Depression
Irritability
Oversleeping
Increased appetite
Fatigue

Nightmares
Difficulty concentrating
Achiness
Anxiety
Suicidal thoughts

I considered walking out. They couldn't make me stay; I was a goddamn adult. Without my pills, I felt unable to focus or follow a thought through to completion. I was no longer rambling but rather introverted, almost shy. I felt numb, sort of out of it. I was so mad at myself for putting myself in this position. The counselor assured me that these symptoms would subside in a matter of days considering the length of time I was addicted wasn't that long. He explained that the duration of the withdrawal depended on the frequency and dose someone takes. People who take larger doses for longer periods of time experience withdrawal symptoms for a longer time.

I guessed this was good news, but while I was in the throes of it, I felt like crap.

I also felt neglectful and self-centered. I wasn't even allowed to call home or receive visitors. It was torture.

I also learned that there are two types of Adderall. I'm not even sure which I was taking. There is regular Adderall and Adderall XR (Extended Release). Regular, which was what I assumed I was on, started working immediately and its effects wore off after several hours. It left the body fairly quickly.

Conversely, Adderall XR built up and stayed in the body longer.

I was pretty sure I wasn't on XR because I started to feel the detox symptoms right away.

Just a few weeks back I couldn't stay in bed because I couldn't wait to get started on the list of things I wanted to accomplish. Now I dreaded getting up.

I felt sluggish and irritable.

Not to mention, I had a headache for a solid day. I struggled to get to group and didn't want to deal with sharing.

I had a roommate who had been here for months already. She seemed nice, but she didn't stop talking.

I appreciated that she was trying to show me the ropes, but my head was pounding and all I could hear was her constant chatter.

I thought she said her name was Patty. Or was it Alison? I didn't even care.

I promised myself I would try to pay attention to her after I got rid of my headache.

Some of the stories that were shared in group were extreme, and I questioned if I even belonged there. The more we went around the room there were a few that mirrored my experience, and I decided it made sense for me to stay.

There was one guy named Troy who couldn't stop crying and was actually on suicide watch. I think he was drunk and killed a kid.

One woman sounded a lot like me. She had felt invisible and was looking for a jolt. She detailed how she started only taking the Adderall on occasion but felt markedly better when she took it and thus the cycle began.

So as the counselors reduced the dose of Adderall to get me fully off it, I went through the process like a zombie. As you could imagine, it got way worse before it got better. I was freezing and then would start to sweat. I felt hopeless a lot of the time, and then just depressed. Finally, at about the three-week mark, I felt able to contribute and saw a glimmer of light at the end of the tunnel.

My roommate Alison, not sure where I got Patty from, had a tough hill to climb. She was a heroin addict who had been clean and had had a relapse. She confided in me that she preferred being in rehab to out in the world. She had a boyfriend who was also an addict, and he wasn't supportive of her getting clean.

As soon as she was released, he would convince her to start using again. She didn't have the strength to resist when she was in the real world, and he took advantage of that.

I felt sad listening to her. I missed Drew and Gary.

I had found my rhythm at rehab and started to feel human again. I contributed on a regular basis and actually made some friends.

There was something really comforting about the mundane chores, the mindless crafts, the countless hours of sharing feelings that made me enjoy rehab. I had my own apprehension about going home.

I spent a lot of time trying to comfort Troy and explain to him that he was sick. Of course, there was no way of escaping the feelings of guilt he had, but I reminded him he didn't do it on purpose. It was an accident, and he had to acknowledge that.

In Alison's case, I tried to understand what she could possibly love about a boyfriend who was trying to keep her addicted to heroin. She admitted it wasn't him exactly, but she had never been on her own before, and once she got out of rehab she had no confidence her family would take her back in. She was like the girl who cried wolf, and they didn't trust her.

However, something happened, and I knew it was time for me to go home. I was almost at the end of my sentence, I mean "stay."

There was one woman named Kristen I really got along with. She was there because she was addicted to a different drug called Klonopin. We spent all our free time together. Well, let me rephrase that. We spent all of our scheduled free time together in art therapy, equestrian therapy, music therapy, cooking therapy and therapy therapy.

If I were being honest, it was like the best camp for adults you could imagine. Despite pouring out your feelings ad nauseum, you got to just be. Of course, it was at will for most of us, but Kristen was mandated by her employer. If she didn't complete the program, she would be out of a job.

One day Kristen pulled me aside and told me she had found a way to score some pills. Someone on the inside was willing to help her get some Klonopin. She quickly explained that she felt they had taken her off it too quickly, and no one was listening to her. She told me that she could probably get me some Adderall if I wanted. I felt so sad listening to her try to rationalize her actions. I was there not too long ago. She was still a friend, and I would need to get away from her. After all, I was newly clean and could easily be tempted to fall back into my old habits.

I had to decide whether to turn her in, which I knew would be the right thing to do, or to stay out of it, which would be the easier thing to do.

I told her I wasn't interested, and I tried to discourage her, reminding her how far we had come. She got a little irritable, telling me she already had a mother.

I didn't want to be a rat, but I thought back on my intervention, and in retrospect I wasn't angry that I had people in my life actually looking out for me.

However, I had a very different relationship with Kristen. I had only known her for four weeks. I decided to sleep on it.

Morning came and I didn't feel any better. I only had two weeks left and then I got to go home.

I decided what I had to do, hoping that Doctor Andy would go along with me. This was very risky because he, of course, had way more to lose than I did. But I thought I would appeal to what was at stake.

I also did my due diligence and found out a little dirt on Doctor Andy.

You know how therapists often become counselors because of something they are trying to overcome? They then feel compelled to devote their lives to helping others in an effort to pay it forward. Well, Mr. Clean-as-a-Whistle Doctor Andy had his own addiction prior to becoming an addiction counselor. He was a gambler. I decided to play the odds, which were clearly in my favor.

His side hustle, aside from lecturing others on how to overcome addiction, was betting. He had been in recovery for numerous years but still had a huge debt that he needed to pay off.

As he appealed to us in the welcome speech upon entering rehab, he shared that he had almost lost his house, his car, and his family due to this weakness.

I thought maybe I would hit him where it hurt and see in my subtle way if I could get him to take some money to ease his financial burden.

I prefaced my conversation with him by ensuring that this fell under the doctor/patient confidentiality clause, and that whatever I told him stayed between us. I knew that when he heard the potential danger Kristen might be in, he might be forced to violate our pact for her safety. I thought I could tell Kristen I sought advice because I was conflicted if, and only if, I got busted for my scheme.

As I told him the situation, I understood once again why I was so successful at sales. I told him how he had changed my life and that if it weren't for this program, I would be down the rabbit hole for sure.

He had a quizzical get-to-the-point look on his face, and I decided to go for it.

By the way, that was all true. I recognized now where I had been heading, and I saw that I was literally spiraling out of control. Which may be why I felt so compelled to help Kristen.

So I told him of my conversation with Kristen, and I said perhaps the way I wanted her to get caught was not ideal for him (Doctor Andy) but it would put my mind at ease and hopefully salvage a really important relationship. I would also want to contribute to his own personal success and make sure that he didn't lose any of the valuable things he referenced in his welcome speech. His house, his car, or his family.

I imagined he had a lot of debt, and I was "indebted" to him, so I suggested a contribution to his fund if he considered that this plan could be executed.

He listened, and I wondered to myself if he played poker. His face didn't move, and I explained how I would like to go back to Kristen and tell her I had changed my mind and would love a few pills before I left.

I would ask her to score me some Adderall and we would "both" get busted. This way she wouldn't know I ratted her out, she got help and I got to go home.

I knew for sure he was totally uncomfortable with the plan, but I also knew he was human and liked me as a person and, frankly, needed the money.

He weighed the pros and cons and replied that he could get in serious trouble if this ever got out.

I said I could imagine, but why would it?

Silence, for what felt like an eternity, and then an OK. He wasn't happy, but he knew it took a lot for me to come forward, which I didn't have to do. Kristen couldn't and shouldn't go backward and if this was how we had to stop her, then we would proceed with extreme caution.

I got that high feeling I always did when I was orchestrating a new project. I went back to Kristen and told her to place my order too.

She smiled, looking relieved that she had a partner in crime. I didn't really feel guilty because I knew why I was doing what I was doing. The only thing that I felt badly about was putting Doctor Andy in an impossible position.

We set up the deal and prepared to pick up the goods behind the kitchen at 8.p.m. One of the cooks agreed to get the pills. I wasn't privy to the particulars of the arrangement, which was just as well. I preferred not to know.

Doctor Andy would coincidentally be responding to an emergency call and catch us in the act and enforce the recommended punishments. For me, it was getting expelled from the program a few days early.

I thought it could really work, Kristen's sobriety wouldn't be compromised, our friendship could remain intact, and no one would be the wiser. I planned on leaving right after this concluded. Doctor Andy would pretend that I was in trouble as well and I would make my exit stage right.

After plotting this, I felt exhausted and homesick. I fully appreciated how lucky I was to be able to afford this program and heal, but I had had enough and wanted to see my family.

Waiting until 8 p.m. was like watching paint dry. Acting "normal" wasn't that hard for me. I realized I had been acting a lot over the past year.

Dinner concluded, we made some stupid birdhouses in art therapy, and we went to pick up the goods. It was easy to go into the kitchen—we just said we were looking for some sweets, which would never happen. Since I was off the Adderall, I was back to counting every calorie.

We met with Javi, the cook, and proceeded out back to make the exchange. That was when it happened. We saw Doctor Andy and realized the jig was up. (Wink, wink).

Doctor Andy asked us what we were doing back there. We both stared and said nothing and then we both started saying different things at the same time. He then asked us what was in the bag. We both said "nothing" simultaneously.

He told us, in a very calm voice, to hand it over. He reminded us that we had both signed waivers that allowed anyone at the facility to search our things at will.

I tried to look as panicked as Kristen was. I was actually a little worried that she would figure out I had leaked the meet-up. She just looked scared. He opened the envelopes and saw the pills. Javi was fired on the spot. He was a casualty of this plan, but he really shouldn't be working at a rehab center if he was willing to sabotage the clientele's sobriety in the first place.

We got taken into the head office and of course got spoken to separately. I ended up expediting my return home. Kristen fell into a major depression and was now committed for an additional six months.

She was crying and muttering that she didn't think she could do this without her Klonopin.

I understood what she was feeling. I wished I could have gone to comfort her, but that would likely have blown my cover. I stayed behind the closed door and planned on reaching out to check on her after I was safely out of the facility.

I made arrangements for Gary to pick me up. I had never wanted to see him as badly as I did now.

The morning I was set to leave Doctor Andy asked me if I wanted to come into his office for one last session. I was grateful to have something to do so I welcomed the opportunity.

He asked me how I was feeling, and I replied that I was very nervous. I thought back on all of the terrible things that had transpired over the last year, and I was horrified. I tried to imagine my reaction if Gary and my roles were reversed. It wasn't good.

Doctor Andy looked at me for a minute.

"What the serious fuck, Claire? I thought you were making such progress but extorting your therapist does not bode well. Unfortunately, you took advantage of my kryptonite. I wish I didn't need the money, but I am trying to dig myself out of a deep hole. I think Kristen needs to be here, so I went against my better judgment, but behavior like this is going to put you right back at where you started. I feel like a walking hypocrite Claire, and I can't imagine you feel much better. This was highly unethical, and I hope that you start making better choices."

I suddenly felt ashamed of what I had done to Doctor Andy. I apologized that I had put him in a no-win situation.

I was apologizing a lot lately.

I don't think he forgave me—I think he just wanted me out, and it was too late for me to fix yet another mess I had caused.

Doctor Andy assured me that everyone had their own cross to bear. I knew that to be true, but this felt self-inflicted, which made it harder to swallow.

He asked me what I loved about Gary. The list was long, but I started telling him about his sense of humor, his patience, the way he celebrated my wins with me and was never jealous, and how he accommodated and accepted my idiosyncrasies.

He asked why this time would be different. I felt slightly better pondering this question.

I was so afraid Gary was going to reject me. I was ashamed of what I had put our family through, and I prayed that he would forgive me.

We had taken marriage vows, for better or worse, in sickness and in health, but how many 20-year-olds really consider what happens over a lifetime?

It wasn't our fault—it was just you don't know what you don't know.

After my talk with Doctor Andy, I went back to my room, gathered my stuff, and thought about how I could explain to Gary how I ended up here. How did I?

When I thought about it, I had just lost my way. I was in a rut at work, Drew was becoming self-sufficient to a degree, Gary was always behind his computer, and I was bored and uninspired.

I didn't think I would ever get addicted. The selling seemed like an easy opportunity, and I had just lost control. As unexciting as that sounded, it was the God's honest truth.

I wished I could take it back, but now hopefully I could move forward. I prayed I would be forgiven.

I wanted to avoid Kristen at all costs. That wasn't going to be difficult since she was holed up in her room, but I couldn't take the chance of running into her.

I was going to miss my roommate Alison. After I got used to her nonstop chatter, she was pretty interesting. I wished she could get away from her loser boyfriend. She was pretty, smart, just in love with a druggie.

No way for me to convince her otherwise, but she had the whole world in front of her.

I worried about Troy. He didn't seem any better to me, just sad. I wondered if he would ever get out of here.

I was standing by the door when I saw my handsome husband approaching. I had butterflies in my stomach.

Gary walked in, we exchanged pleasantries and I lost it and held onto him for dear life. He was equally emotional, which made me feel like I still had a chance. I asked where Drew was, and Gary explained that he asked him if he could take the flight and drive alone to gather his thoughts and allow us time to talk.

I immediately thought he was going to ask for a divorce. He wouldn't want to do that in front of Drew.

We made small talk as we loaded up the car, but once inside I decided to spill my guts.

I explained to him that everything had started out fine, and I was just looking to get some of my vim and vigor back. I was feeling bored with work, Drew was doing his own thing, he seemed preoccupied, and I was looking to get some excitement back into my life. It wasn't meant to be an everyday thing, but when I realized how good I felt I didn't want to go back into the doldrums. Then I realized that it was taking more and more to get me to that happy place, and it spiraled out of control.

He looked at me with those sad eyes and asked how he had missed all this.

I told him not to blame himself and that I had purposely deceived him, had put on an act, and then just got lost.

He asked me about the selling part.

"Gary, when have I done anything half-assed?" I replied.

I told him that I felt guilty about spending our money on drugs so I thought if I didn't have to pay for them that would justify it. Then my overactive mind saw some potential to help the other moms and make a buck.

He was quiet.

I was quiet.

Then I asked him about giving me the smoothies and whether he knew I was having troubles in the bedroom. He looked dumbfounded.

"Not everything is about you, Claire," he said angrily. "What issues are you talking about?"

Oh Jesus, now I had to get into that. Why didn't I keep my big mouth shut?

It was too late for me to recant so I said in addition to the Adderall mess I had developed some sexual dysfunction as well. I told him that I was still attracted to him but noticed I was experiencing some symptoms that were making it hard for me to, you know?

"I *don't* know, and can you please just finish a sentence?"

I told him I was having trouble orgasming and was trying to fix it on my own. So I had bought a zillion lubes and supplements that were supposed to help, and I was being more aggressive in the bedroom to see if they were working.

And then I told him that was why I thought he was making me smoothies. He smiled a little, and said he was just trying to be healthier and then wanted to know why I didn't come to him and talk about it.

He told me that we were always supposed to tell each other everything and get through things together. How did the two of us get so far apart?

It was a valid question. One I couldn't answer.

Gary

I couldn't believe I had the gene. I heard the doctor say it, I saw it on paper, but I had been feeling so good it made no sense. Just because I had the mutation didn't mean I had cancer, but it pretty much means I will.

I felt sort of guilty, but the first person I wanted to reach out to was Jean. Next Henri. Why wasn't it Claire?

I sent a message to Jean and told her I got the results back and they weren't good.

She responded instantaneously and said she was so sorry and asked me if I had told Claire.

Now I had to explain to her that I had planned on telling Claire but that she ended up in rehab.

Jean responded, "Gary, you can't deal with this on your own. It's a lot to handle."

I totally agreed, but I needed Claire to focus on her demons first and get them at bay. Her rehab program was six weeks. I planned on telling her as soon as she was home. In the meantime, I had to be here for Drew, since he had to process that his mother was addicted to drugs and selling them to his school's PTA.

I felt for the kid.

Jean said that when Claire got back and settled, I should take a little trip to stay with her in Canada.

She wished the circumstances were better but she and Loretta could tell me more about our dad and help me deal with the news I had just received. This would also give Claire an opportunity to repair the relationship between her and Drew.

I replied immediately that I would like to take her up on that.

I hadn't expected Claire to have to go off to rehab but I could still plan my scans and take care of the first round of screenings while she was away.

I decided I wasn't going to tell her until she got home, and then there was the matter of getting Drew tested.

I knew I should schedule his tests immediately, but I couldn't imagine doing it before Claire got out.

I didn't even recognize my wife anymore.

I was having a harder time getting my brain around the fact that she was selling drugs. What was this, "Breaking Bad?" My wife had turned into Walter White aka Heisenberg.

I was angry. I was sure she was going to be equally pissed when she learned I had kept the Li-Fraumeni Syndrome from her, especially because it could potentially affect our son.

In my defense, I was going to tell her that I wanted to shield her from the anxiety I was feeling. I thought I would actually be able to say, "Dodged a bullet, huh?"

Anyway, this was about her right now. Selling drugs to PTA moms? Taking pills multiple times a day? What happened to the woman who made me go to multiple supermarkets to find organic chickens?

The house definitely was missing something while she was at rehab. Not to mention, I was sick of cereal and smoothies. I had to cave and have some processed food. I guess I had taken for granted the meals that were always just waiting for me at mealtime.

They didn't just magically appear, which I forgot. Same with the laundry getting done, groceries being stocked and Drew making it to the orthodontist, baseball practice, honor's society meetings and driver's ed without me even knowing.

I thought we could get past this, but we had both been so deceitful. I was itching to get to Canada, but now I would have to wait. I would pick up Claire, confide in her about the diagnosis, and head off to Canada to take some space and let her get reacclimated.

I decided it might be time to tell Henri.

I grabbed my iPad but didn't how to begin. I didn't want to freak him out, but now I thought he really should make plans to be tested.

I started out with the usual "Hi, bro."

"Bro, it's good to hear from you."

I cut right to the chase. "The results came back, and I have the mutation."

Nothing for several minutes, and then he said he felt pain in his heart. I told him the same thing I had been repeating to myself: This didn't mean I have cancer but that I had to be diligent with screenings and be careful about exposure to radiation.

He told me that I made a good point. He then asked me if I had told Jean. I said that I had, and that she had invited me to stay with her for a little bit.

Then I realized I hadn't told him about Claire. He told me that would be good for me, and would Claire go with me?

Next, I told about Claire going into rehab and the whole Adderall fiasco. Maybe he could share his perspective with me.

I asked him if he knew what Adderall was.

He told me some U.S. prescriptions are actually considered illegal narcotics in Europe, such as Adderall and other stimulant drugs used to treat ADHD/ADD.

Even if a U.S. doctor prescribed these medications legally in the U.S. that wouldn't fly in Europe, he added.

I asked what happened if your kid had ADHD. You'd have to move?

He said, no, they have a drug similar called Concerta. Its effect is milder than those of amphetamines, which was what Adderall was considered.

He then told me he was sorry for me and Claire.

I told him I was angry that she had done this to our family.

He asked me if I smoked, which I thought was a weird reply, but I said no, that my adoptive father had emphysema and cirrhosis of the liver, so I was never inclined to start.

Henri told me he smoked from when he was 15 to 50 and was 10 years without any cigarettes, but there wasn't a day that went by without thinking about smoking one. Now the smell actually made him ill, he said, but addiction was a hard thing. He told me he was praying for me and for Claire.

Then he asked me if I had spoken to Claire about my diagnosis.

I said we hadn't spoken and that she had gone straight to rehab after we did an intervention, and they weren't allowed phones or visits until the program concluded.

He asked me how it was without her in the house. I said it was quiet and sort of lonely. I told him that I had been so preoccupied with my history and the gene that I had sort of been checked out.

He asked if she was feeling, how do you say, "neglected?"

He made a good point.

Claire

As we made our way home, there was an obvious tension. We were definitely happy to see each other, but there was also an elephant in the room. I started telling him I hoped he knew just how sorry I truly was. I wasn't being cavalier when making my decisions, I said, I just didn't realize how things were snowballing and I would regret it for the rest of my life.

Gary didn't respond for a few minutes, which felt like hours. He said he knew I had no intention of getting into this situation, but it was really hard for him to pretend he could just put it behind him.

He raised his voice and said, "You sold drugs, Claire. I just can't fathom that this seemed like a good idea, even for a split second, and yet it went on for almost a year."

"Well, when you put it like that, it sounds terrible. I just didn't really think that Adderall was a *drug, drug.*"

"Well, look at where you landed."

I told him I didn't know how many different ways I could apologize, but that I couldn't take it back and wished that I could for so many reasons. The biggest was his disappointment in me. Having Drew feel ashamed of his mother was a close second, I told him.

"I'm not perfect," I said. "But then haven't you ever done anything you wished you could take back?"

Suddenly Gary looked really uncomfortable.

Now that I mentioned it, he said, there was something he had to tell me.

Automatically, I assumed he had had an affair while I was at rehab. My heart sank. As I waited for him to say it, he started rambling on about Ancestry.

Way to change the subject.

I asked directly if he was cheating on me.

We were having two totally different conversations. He said that he was telling me he had found out about his father—and that he had never cheated on me.

"When did you find him?" I asked.

Gary turned stark white and said it was now his turn to apologize. There was a lot that he had been waiting to tell me and he had thought of even keeping it in longer to make sure I was stable. But he thought it had to be told.

He proceeded to tell me about the Li-Fraumeni Syndrome, which I had never heard of, and how three of his sisters were deceased. Then the bomb dropped. He told me that he went for genetic testing—behind my back, I will add—and has the gene.

"WTF, Gary?" I exclaimed. "How could you keep that from me, and what about Drew?"

He started tearing up and told me he was sorry, that he would have been annoyed if I had kept it from him. He had just assumed he wouldn't have it. The good news was that while I was at rehab he went for scans and the scans were clean. The bad news, he said, was that we would have to get Drew tested.

We boarded the plane, and both of us were caught up in our own thoughts.

When we got home and I first saw Drew, I was overcome with the love I felt for him. How could I have jeopardized our life together?

We embraced and went inside and tried to resume some sort of normalcy.

A few days went by and the tension in the air was palpable. It seemed that both Gary and I were feeling extreme emotions at different points. There were times that I was so remorseful and appreciative of the two men in my life I just cried. Conversely, I was so pissed off about all of the things Gary had hidden from me I couldn't even talk to him.

Gary

The atmosphere in the house was really stressful. I was so happy that Claire had completed her stint in rehab, and I thought she was really doing better. She wasn't manic so I could tell she was no longer taking anything. We were just having a hard time communicating. I knew she was angry with me for keeping the Li-Fraumeni Syndrome details from her, and I was equally unhappy with her drug ring. We both had a lot to overcome. I wanted to take that trip to visit Jean.

The timing made total sense. Claire could take this time to get back into a "normal" routine and connect with Drew. I, on the other hand, wanted to meet my half-sisters and take some time to figure out what would happen next.

I decided to give Jean a call and see if my invitation was still good. She confirmed that it was but forewarned me that she was in the midst of chemo and wasn't feeling her best. She was tired much of the time, so she said as long as I didn't need to be entertained, I was welcome.

Of course I didn't need to be entertained, but I considered asking Loretta if perhaps I should stay with her or get a hotel room.

Regardless of where I stayed, it was agreed that I would be coming for an extended visit.

I wasn't sure how Claire was going to take the news, but I would do my best to assure her that it had more to do with me spending time with my sisters than our relationship. Even though our relationship didn't feel that solid to me right now.

I wasn't innocent here, but we were just so disconnected. I was hoping the time away would make my heart grow fonder, although she had just been away for six weeks.

I thought perhaps we should consider this a trial separation. Not that things were that bad, but if I did have cancer, I could spare her the agony of all of the treatments and I could just deal with it on my own. I was going to soul-search with Jean and Loretta, but I felt so sad.

Claire

I wasn't home two minutes and Gary was taking a trip to visit his sisters. Not to be self-centered, but what about me? I have always been strong and managed my own shit, but I really needed to lean on him to help me with my sobriety.

It was easy in rehab since you were monitored pretty much 24/7.

I was just afraid that when left to my own devices, I might slip up. I thought I would try and find a center nearby that helped people with their addictions.

If Gary wasn't going to be there for me, I would find another support system. Wow, in 30 years he had always been my person. Did I do this to us?

I looked for an outpatient facility. I had been away from Drew for too long and felt like I had to mend some fences. He was really a mature kid and was checking on me constantly.

I felt guilty that I had made him grow up so quickly. He would never forget his mom was an addict—coupled with me compromising the parents of his friends. That saying "don't shit where you eat" was exactly what I had done.

He didn't seem to hold it against me, recognizing that I was temporarily insane.

I called the number for Reclaim You, the addiction center not too far from where we lived. I spoke to a lovely woman but learned that this wasn't covered completely by my insurance, which didn't make any sense.

My first thought was to sell some Adderall to cover the costs.

Clearly, I needed to be there.

I was still out on disability for another month. There were several programs I got to choose from, but I decided the full-day program made the best sense. I was afraid to have any time on my hands but wanted to be home when Drew got home from school so we could spend the evenings together and salvage our tenuous relationship.

I arrived at 7:30 a.m. and completed an intake interview. Even though they knew my story, this helped them structure my customized treatment plan. At 8 a.m. I ate breakfast with my assigned group. Of course, everyone was really shy so it was a bit awkward. Then we all went into our first session.

We went around the room and introduced ourselves and explained why we were there. Some of the stories were so much worse than mine I started thinking maybe I didn't need to be there. Then I remembered my son was taking care of me, and my husband was in another country.

When it was my turn and I told my story one kid said, "Shit you sold drugs in your son's school, that slaps."

I realized I definitely belonged.

We were given a break to journal and then we went to individual therapy. I was so sick of telling my story, but it was critical for me to figure out how I got here.

The therapist asked what had prompted me to start taking Adderall. I explained how I had heard about it from Lynn when I mentioned to her that I was feeling trapped. Rather than calling out Lynn, she started to ask me what I meant by "feeling trapped."

I replied in an angry tone that I didn't know, I was just feeling sort of invisible. What was my purpose? My kid was grown, my job was repetitive and boring, I was starting to feel old and useless like I didn't shine anymore.

She said it was interesting that I took for granted that I had raised an independent son who was flourishing. That I have had a successful career for decades and have contributed to my household to afford a very nice life, that I have had an equally long marriage that sounds like up until now was quite loving and happy.

Then she asked what success looked like to me.

I let those words marinate. What was my problem? Was I a narcissist who needed attention? Why did I need to always stand out?

I didn't really have an answer, but these were things I had never thought about.

That 90-minute session went by in a split second.

Next, we did a fitness session, which I didn't feel like doing. I chose a spin class, and I hadn't been on the Peloton in close to a year. If I hadn't been exhausted before the class, I was done and dusted after it.

I couldn't wait to go back to my room.

I still had one more educational session before the day concluded. The session was actually on nutrition, which apparently can help manage the stress of recovery and even curb withdrawal cravings.

I was finally done with the day, but before I left the class I texted Drew and asked him if he would like to go out to dinner.

He quickly responded that he didn't want to but would love to get takeout and eat at home.

I was relieved. I thought he didn't want to spend time with me so I quickly agreed and went to pick up some sushi so we could catch up and I could learn about what he had been up to in my absence.

Drew

This was so weird. I was trying really hard to be strong and not show my mom how freaked out I was by the fact that she had sold drugs at my school. The stares and whispers behind my back sucked big time. I was going to ask this girl Lainey I like to the prom, but knowing that her mom was in the PTA I decided not to. I was sure my mother was notorious among those moms, and I didn't want to have to deal with even more rumors.

It was a bummer because I thought Lainey was pretty and smart, and I felt like she would say yes.

I longed for the day I got to leave for college and get away from both of my parents. My dad was totally on another planet lately. He sometimes looked at me and got teary-eyed for no reason.

If he was sad that I was going to be leaving for college, why was he wasting the time he had left with me blubbering?

I wasn't sure why my mother had gone off the deep end. I wanted to ask her, but I didn't want to trigger her.

When she got home with the sushi, I suggested we eat while watching a movie so we didn't have to talk.

She said she wanted to talk rather than watch a movie. She had been gone six weeks and wanted to hear what I had been up to.

"Really, mom?" I blurted out. "You want to know what I have been up to? I have been spending tons of time trying to figure out why you started selling drugs at my school. How about that?

I have been trying to avoid my friends so that I don't have to dodge questions that I haven't the slightest idea how to answer. How could you do this to our family? I want to feel badly for you, but I am mad. This is my senior year. It's supposed to be my time."

She started to cry.

"Drew, you and dad are the most important people in my life. I don't really know how I am going to make it up to you or how I can convey my remorse. I am so deeply sorry. I am going to rehab to try and understand what perpetuated this behavior, but I can't undo it. So, if you could find it in your heart to be mad, but also forgive me, I would be so grateful. I will spend every day forward trying to make it up to you."

"I know it wasn't on purpose, but it's just going to take some time."

My mom looked sad.

"How about we watch that movie? I will wait however long it takes."

Claire

I had never felt such pain, knowing that Drew was ashamed of me. If I ever had a reason to stay sober, it was this. He could barely look at me. I was in shambles.

The center I was going to, Reclaim You, was definitely making a difference. I didn't have to wonder about how I was going to fill my day, and I was coming to terms with some of my feelings.

My therapist suggested I reach out to Brian and tie up that loose end.

I dreaded it, but I did owe him that since I had sent him further down a bad path.

I texted him, and said, "Hey, can we catch up?"

Nothing for minutes and then in his usual way, he wrote back, "Yah."

"Five Guys?" I replied.

He said he would see me there. I asked if we could make it at 6 p.m. because I was on a roll and didn't want to miss therapy.

I spent my day preoccupied with the pending conversation playing over and over in my head. I had to trust that when I saw him it would just come out.

Finally, it was time. I got out of the car and immediately spotted Brian.

"Hello," I said, "it's nice to see you."

"You too," was his curt reply.

We ordered and sat down.

"Look, Brian, I am really sorry. I am an adult, and what I got you involved with is reprehensible and I am ashamed."

"I am still selling to your moms and now I cut out the middleman, you. I'm not upset at all."

"Brian, you have to stop, this is a felony and a terrible journey for you to pursue."

"You do you, and I will take care of me."

That was all.

I decided that I was barely making it myself, so I wasn't going to try and change him. I left by saying I wished he would consider coming to Reclaim You with me.

He thanked me.

"We're good, gotta roll."

That was all of the closure I would get for now. I was truly exhausted.

Gary

I tried to reassure Claire that this trip to Canada to visit my sisters wasn't about us, but rather me learning more about my ancestry and figuring out how I was going to deal with this health situation that I would be plagued with for the rest of my life.

She reminded me that she was part of the rest of my life, and then there was the matter of Drew.

She was right, I couldn't keep putting off his test and waiting wouldn't guarantee better results.

I agreed that we should do that before I went. I still thought I would like to have some space, so I rented a cheap apartment close by until I knew what was going to happen with us.

She said if we were going to work on our relationship, did I really think being apart was the way to do it?

I told her I wasn't sure I wanted to work on our relationship. I would always love her, I said, but what she did was hard to swallow.

She looked sad, and I felt terrible.

I said that right now I had been given a death sentence and that was all I could focus on. That and the fact that I may have passed this along to our son.

Let's get him tested, I said, and then we can discuss what happens next with our relationship. It is a month-to-month lease, just temporary for now.

I called the same doctor that did my test and he got Drew in for the following week. We had to sit down and tell Drew about what was going on, which might be the hardest thing I have ever had to do in my life.

We made a plan to all have dinner, and Claire and I were on the same page about being transparent. We would let him know the odds, which were high, since I had it and what that would mean, but also reminded him that since we were screening him early and frequently this was manageable. We would try and keep him distracted until the results came in, but I knew how that worked in my case. It might be easier since he had both of us to at least listen to his concerns.

I was reminded once again that I shouldn't have left Claire out of my diagnosis. That was unfair to both of us, and stupid on my part.

Claire made one of her amazing meals, which I was now appreciating, and I was happy we were together.

"Buddy, I owe you an apology," I told Drew. "I have been distracted lately, and you could have really used me to be present. Your mother was dealing with her situation, and you were sort of left to your own devices, but I want to tell you what is going on."

He looked concerned but continued to listen.

I told him about Ancestry, and we laughed about Arthur Murray, and then I told him about my sisters and my father and the gene.

He looked so afraid, and I felt like crying, but I knew I couldn't show him my fear.

"Hey, we are going to face this head on and do whatever has to be done together," I told him in a strong voice. "You are not alone."

He asked me about the odds of him getting it, and I told him I wouldn't lie to him. There was a 50 percent chance.

He then asked to be excused and I wanted to hug him, but I knew I needed to be alone after I learned too so Claire and I said in unison that that was fine.

I felt so guilty. There was nothing I could have done differently. Would I not have had children if I knew the risk?

If I was honest, knowing how different my relationship was with Drew compared with my relationship with my adoptive parents, selfishly I probably would have still wanted to have a biological child even knowing the risks. This was a high price to pay.

Drew

All of a sudden, I went from having the coolest parents to the most fucked-up parents on the planet.

What was happening? This was supposed to be the best year of my life and my parents weren't getting along, I could have a genetic mutation and my dad was heading to Canada to find himself.

They had always been there for me and now I felt like I had no one.

I thought I was going to ask Lainey out. I didn't want to get involved because of the whole mom PTA thing, but I felt like I needed a friend. Why not make it a cute one?

I was nervous but decided to go for it. I didn't have much to lose.

I obviously didn't want to dump all of my stuff on her, but it would be nice to have someone to talk to.

My friend Brad had her number, so I texted her first to see what type of response I got.

"Hey Lainey, what's up?"

"Hi Drew, nice to hear from you."

I was encouraged.

"I was wondering if you would like to hang out some time."

My heart was beating out of my chest.

"I would like that."

"Cool."

"Yeah, cool."

I went from feeling lower than low to feeling a little excited. True, my parents might divorce, and I could have a syndrome I couldn't even pronounce but I also had a date!

I decided that was enough for one night, I didn't want her to think I was too into her. So I texted "deets to follow."

Was "deets" stupid? Too late, I couldn't un-text it. I had to try and sound more chill in my next exchange.

We ended up making plans for the following Saturday night.

I told my parents I had a date, and they were so worried about me that they asked If I needed a ride, offered me money, and told me no curfew, they trusted me.

We met at the mall because neither one of us drove, which was pushing me to get my permit. I hadn't really cared one way or the other about learning to drive, but now I felt motivated.

We decided on dinner and a movie. We went to a little bistro, which was cute but within my budget. We started with small talk and I asked her if she knew where she was going to college, and I asked about her interests in music, sports, and other things. Time was flying by. She was so easy to talk to.

I wanted to keep talking but I had bought tickets to the movie, so I paid the check and we left. I wanted to hold her hand, but I wasn't sure if I should grab it, or if I would start sweating, so I decided after I bought the popcorn, I would wipe my hands on some napkins and then during the movie I would take her hand.

I totally wasn't paying attention to the movie. I was trying to figure out where to put the popcorn and how I could subtly hold her hand. I hoped we didn't have to discuss the movie because at this point, I didn't even know the plot. I realized we were halfway through, and I was going to have to make my move.

I went for it, and her hand relaxed into mine. It was so awesome. The armrest was in my way, but I wasn't going to shift for fear of disrupting the vibe.

This was one of the best nights of my life. I felt hopeful and excited. I thought about telling my parents about Lainey and then I remembered who they were now. My old parents would have been so excited for me. Who knows how these shells of my former parents would react or if they would even care.

I wasn't letting their shit spoil my night. I was going to hold onto this.

Claire

I wished time would speed up and we had insight into what Drew's health future looked like. Even after the test, it would take three weeks to get the results. Gary decided that he was going to Canada for those three weeks.

At first, I thought that was insane but after thinking about it I realized that if God forbid Drew had the gene,

Gary would never want to leave his side, let alone the country. Second, we were hovering over

Drew like he was breakable, and I was sure we were annoying him.

So it might be best if Gary weren't here and we tried to keep busy until the results were in.

Gary wasn't the only one who was mad. He was making it seem like I did what I did intentionally, which I didn't. Meanwhile, he blatantly hid the Li-Fraumeni Syndrome from me for almost two months. That wasn't exactly holding up our vows either.

Let him go to Canada. I needed to be diligent with my therapy and continue to work my program while trying to be available for Drew.

I wished Gary a good trip and tried not to let my anger seep out. Perhaps the space would do us good. Of course, I was distraught that he had this gene, and I planned on being with him as he navigated the future, but why the hell would he cut me out of this major life event? We had been stuck like glue for close to 30 years.

I remembered reading an article in a women's magazine where the author proposed a renewable marriage contract every five years. At the end of each of those five years, you would get to either renew or cancel your contract.

Were Gary and I expiring?

There were so many great things about our dynamic, but we had definitely hit a rough patch. I had to evaluate the hassle-to-fun ratio and decide if I wanted to continue to fight for us. Either way, I wouldn't let him battle the syndrome alone.

It boggled my mind that I would even consider us separating. However, I didn't want to continue forward the way we were interacting now. I was walking on eggshells, mad, sad, and tense. Worst part was I couldn't even take an antidepressant. I just cracked myself up.

Enough of this pity party, I was getting on my bike and sweating out my anxiety. I was going to see if Drew would go out to dinner with me somewhere. We needed to go out so that we didn't end up eating in front of the TV again. Usually if I offered steak, he would indulge me.

Gary

I loaded up the car and prepared for my drive to Ontario.

Drew's spirits were markedly improved compared with the other day. I was proud of the way he was handling what was going on.

I assured him that I would be back for the results and just really wanted to get to know my biological family a little bit.

He said it was all fine and he was good. I told him I was glad, but asked him what had changed since the other day?

He just said he had had time to process things and there was no use worrying about things he had no control over.

I found Claire and told her I was about to hit the road. I also told her I loved her, but I really wanted to learn about my family—so she shouldn't read into anything.

She was a little standoffish but wished me well and reminded me to be home before the results came back.

I assured her it was top of mind. We embraced for a minute and off I went.

I thought she would have been trying to convince me to stay, but that didn't happen.

Well, that was good actually. I didn't want to have any distractions while I was with Jean and Loretta. I spoke to Loretta and she let me know that Jean really wasn't responding to the chemo as well as she had done the previous times.

Although I didn't want to be in Jean's way, I didn't want to postpone the trip in case this was my only opportunity to meet her. Things didn't sound good.

On the drive, I spent a lot of time reflecting. Life was hard. So much good, but lots of struggles. I thought about a different life perhaps in Canada. Where would that have led me? I have loved my life with Claire, and honestly Drew was my heart, but this last year had really taken the wind out of my sails. I wondered if we could ever get back to where we were.

There was never a time I could remember when she wasn't part of every waking thought. Suddenly, she was an afterthought.

It was the drugs. It went against everything I stood for. I knew she was trying, but it might just be too late. Then I thought about how she said she would go to screenings with me even though I told her I had rented the apartment. That was a partner. I felt so conflicted. She had always made me feel supported.

Didn't I owe her that?

I guess I was feeling like this was a self-inflicted situation versus my medical condition, which I had no control over.

Drew

Lainey and I had been dating for two weeks, and I had barely thought about the test results. Maybe a little bit at night, but my thoughts were filled with her. We were going to dinner and then to see a band. I thought it was time I confided in her about what I was dealing with. I already knew I liked her, but it was early enough in our relationship that she could tell me it was too much and I would be OK.

I did have friends I played baseball with and met at the park for a scrimmage, but I wouldn't really pull one of them aside to talk about my feelings.

We ordered our meals and I told Lainey that it was really cool she didn't hold the whole PTA thing with my mom against me.

She said she could only imagine how badly it must suck having to deal with all of the backlash.

I nodded and said it did, but I had something bigger on my mind. Suddenly, I was spilling my guts to Lainey about my parents not getting along, and my dad and the gene, and then me possibly having the gene.

She was pale as a ghost. Should I not have told her?

She said that of course I should have told her—I'm her boyfriend. I missed her next few sentences—she said "boyfriend." Yes!

I refocused and said I knew it was a lot but I really had no one to talk to and I was kind of freaked out.

She grabbed my hand and said, "Well, now you have me."

I had another week to wait for the results, I told her, and she said she thought it was messed up that my dad left after my mom had just gotten home.

She then asked what would happen if I had the gene.

I said, from what I understood, I would just have to constantly be checked, like every three months, so if I did have any signs, I could proactively start treating it.

She quickly said that we shouldn't worry about that until we knew. And then she said she would be there for me so I wasn't alone.

I paid the bill, and we headed over to see the band and continued to have another blissful night. I couldn't believe holding someone's hand could make me feel so euphoric.

I was totally going to kiss her tonight. I was taking my permit test tomorrow. I couldn't believe we needed a ride.

I had to make my move before my mommy picked us up. The worst!

I was nervous as hell, but I turned to her and moved a strand of hair off her face, and she looked into my eyes, and it happened. I think I might have seen stars. I wasn't quite sure if I would get it right, but it was just so natural and it seemed that she was happy too.

My mom picked us up, and we dropped Lainey off. As we headed back to our house, she asked if I would have dinner with her tomorrow night. Steak.

She only offered steak when she really wanted my company. Who was I to turn down a nice filet mignon?

I said sure, that would be nice.

Gary

The drive to Canada was uneventful, which was definitely what I needed. I listened to a lot of Yacht rock and sang my heart out.

When I got to the border, I had to show my proof of citizenship and identity, but I had dual citizenship. I was home again.

On my travels I passed through Woodstock, Albany, Syracuse, Rochester and Buffalo. There are some beautiful natural sights like the Hudson Valley and Niagara Falls.

I tried to find peace in appreciating the nature, but I kept thinking why me?

I was a rule follower, had called my parents every week, paid my taxes, never strayed in my marriage—why did I have to deal with this shit?

It was very hard to keep my faith when these unexplainable curve balls came from left field. I thought why not give this gene to a murderer? A philanderer? A rapist?

There was no answer, but this was what was keeping me up at night.

I wasn't saying I had had a bad life by any means, but being adopted was difficult. You couldn't help in most cases but feel different. You couldn't help but continue to wonder why someone who carried you for nine months would give you up.

Then, at least in my case, I was constantly trying to figure out why my adoptive parents went through a year and a half filling out paperwork, traveling to Canada to bring me home, and then virtually ignored me.

Don't get me wrong, it wasn't all bad, but it certainly wasn't good. I was scared of them. They were disappointed easily and never really exhibited joy.

They didn't encourage me to play sports or help me foster any other interests. They didn't seem excited about anything, but rather just existed. In fact, I don't even think they liked each other. What a horrible way to go through life.

I was about 20 minutes away from Jean's house, and I really wanted to stop these ruminating thoughts.

I cranked up Steely Dan and drove the final stretch.

When I got to Jean's, the door was open and the house was just what I had pictured. A little colonial in a nice suburb in Carleton Place, Ontario.

Jean and her husband, William, came out to greet me. I immediately searched her face looking for resemblance and I felt compelled to hug her. She hugged back. I shook William's hand, and he told me to call him Bill.

She was a tiny woman, maybe 5 feet tall. I am an average height of 5' 10." I couldn't stop staring and searching for my history in her eyes.

After I got over the initial shock of where I was, I saw that she looked really tired. She was all smiles, but I could tell she was putting in a lot of effort to make me feel welcome.

I hadn't eaten in hours. The house smelled heavenly, and Jean said they didn't eat this often but she thought she would serve me Poutine, since it was one of the specialties of Canada.

It was a plate of French fries topped with cheese curds and gravy.

I had been subsisting on smoothies and salad, so I dug in with a vengeance. They look pleased.

They asked about the drive, and we talked about our families. I told them that we were waiting on Drew's results.

I had decided I wasn't going to bring up the fact that they didn't get their kids tested, but suddenly I couldn't help myself.

I told them that I understood if they didn't want to answer.

Jean told me that when your children are in their 30s, you can't really insist on anything. They know as many of the facts as she does, and both of them decided they didn't want to know.

I didn't agree with the decision, but it wasn't up to me. I could say that with certainty because I was in their shoes.

Jean looked really exhausted, and I was too—from the emotions, the drive, my life. I thanked them for hosting me, and they showed me to my room.

Claire

I was so excited to be having dinner with my boy. Things at Reclaim You were going very well. I was starting to have hope again, something that had been missing for quite some time.

I asked Drew how he had been doing. I acknowledged that he had a lot to deal with in a very short time.

He told me he was doing pretty good, and then he updated me on how things had been going with Lainey. I was excited, but it was just another milestone to check off. Up until now, I had been the only female in his life.

Of course, I wanted him to find love and experience every amazing thing life had to offer, it was just that another chapter was closing.

I got out of my own head and asked him to tell me all about her. All of a sudden, I realized who Lainey was. She was the daughter of Ginger from the PTA. I was relieved that she wasn't a customer and was thrilled she was so straitlaced. Only a few months back, I was annoyed that Ginger wasn't having anything to do with my Adderall.

He told me Lainey played tennis, they liked the same music, and had been dating almost three weeks. He seemed so excited, and my heart was bursting.

I told him that this was so good for him, especially now.

He took a bite of his steak.

"Do you want to talk about the gene or anything?" I asked him.

"No, I don't want to talk about the gene. I want to talk about what's going on with you and Dad.

"You guys have always been a package deal, wherever you are he is, and vice versa. Now you are never together, and you don't even seem to be talking. Why is this happening?"

It was time for the truth.

"That's a great question, Drew. One I have spent many sleepless nights trying to answer," I said.

"I guess your dad and I are both at a crossroads in our lives. We are caring for our parents, you are almost off to college, we are more than three-quarters of the way through our careers, and it just feels like an ending. I can only speak for myself, but I don't want this phase to end. I was grasping at straws to make time stop and feel more needed. In the process of trying to make that happen, which you know is impossible, I went off track.

Dad, on the other hand, has always had a void because he was adopted. I think when he began the search, he didn't plan on really getting any questions answered. Even when responses came in, they weren't around health. So, it was fun knowing that he had a cousin in PEI, and that his mom was one of four girls, but when he found out about his dad, he felt all sorts of terrible things. Remorse for a family life he was denied. Anger about this stupid gene, sadness that he has all of these siblings so far away, and confusion about how this will play out, and lastly fear of what this means for you.

We should have been communicating like we have always done. For whatever reason, we weren't honest with each other and now there is a chasm.

I'm not sure if it can be mended. I know that I am equally responsible for our demise, but your dad is treating me like a criminal and not admitting, at least to me, that he is at fault too.

He keeps claiming he was trying to spare me. He is no martyr. When you take vows for better or for worse, sharing hard things is covered under that umbrella.

That hurt me deeply. I am trying to understand why he felt the need to protect me, when we have a 30-year history of sharing everything.

So only time will tell how this sorts itself out. Rehab is helping me to understand that I have to take responsibility for my actions, but then I need to forgive myself.

I didn't do anything on purpose, and I would never intentionally hurt the people whom I love the most.

I am hoping that dad gets some closure from spending time with his sisters, but we shall see.

No matter what happens between us, we are both committed to loving you. We will always be your parents and I can say unequivocally that you have been our greatest joy. So, let's try to enjoy this amazing meal, and concentrate on continuing to talk about everything. I love you, son."

He hugged me and I knew he loved me too.

Drew

I was really glad I got to hang out with my mom. It sort of felt like how things used to be between us. Thank God she didn't give me the safe sex talk. Although I was hoping when my dad got home, I could ask him a few questions. I dreaded that too, but much better to ask him than her.

I was afraid to Google anything for fear of getting a virus on my computer, but I did have a few questions. Things were moving along with Lainey, and I didn't want to fumble or look like I didn't know what I was doing. But I didn't know what I was doing.

Lainey always let me talk about how scared I was about the prospect of having this gene. I also had started to think about that fact that my dad did have it. Was he going to get cancer?

She didn't say the usual "everything is going to be fine." I knew she was really considering what it might mean for me and for my dad.

She told me I couldn't do anything until I knew what I was dealing with. She was so wise beyond her years.

Only a few more days until I got the results and my dad came home. I asked her if she had considered not dating me when she found out about what my future might look like.

She told me that everyone has some skeleton in their closet. I asked her what hers was. She was really quiet.

I told her that she could tell me anything.

She said OK but after hearing what she was going to tell me I might not want to date her anymore.

"Sometimes, when I eat too much, I make myself throw up," she said. "I have been caught a few times, and I am trying so hard not to do it, but it makes me feel better. I know it sounds really gross, but my mom is so perfect, and I get really stressed out about keeping up my grades, tennis, friends, so sometimes I binge on food and then throw up."

I never saw that coming. I hugged her. I told her how beautiful she was and she started to cry. And I told her I would try to help and that now we had each other to lean on.

"I love you, Lainey," I said.

She smiled. "I love you too, Drew.

Gary

I slept like a baby last night. I was sure that the drive and those French fries were just the perfect sleep aid.

I looked at my watch and it was 10 a.m. I couldn't believe it. I hadn't slept this late since becoming a father.

I went into the kitchen and Jean and Bill were having eggs and coffee and offered me a plate.

Loretta was going to be coming over, she said, and we thought we would just spend the day, showing me some photo albums and talking if that sounded good.

It sounded perfect.

After I finished my eggs and toast, I said I hoped it was OK that I was asking but that she didn't seem angry when she talked about our father, and he seemed like a real jerk. He had left her family, Henri's family, my mom and spread this mutation to five of his kids.

"Why don't you hate him?" I asked.

Jean said she does have anger toward him, but that anger fuels her cancer. She couldn't waste any more time on him.

She didn't know him well enough to hate him but when she thinks of all the running he did, he just seemed like a lost soul who couldn't find happiness.

Jean decided to lie down a little before Loretta came, and Bill and I walked down to the little pond they had in their backyard.

I told Bill that I had kept the entire genetic testing and diagnosis from Claire and that she was incredibly angry with me.

This gene was a son of a bitch and a game-changer, he told me, and he didn't think I should try to navigate this journey on my own.

He then relayed how hard Jean had been fighting her illness for five years. This last round had been different, and the prognosis wasn't good. The chemo didn't seem to be working, and she was much more lethargic than previous times.

He told me he had a hard time imagining life without her but he would stay by her side. Sometimes having that partner was the impetus one needed to keep fighting, he said.

I appreciated his words and understood why Claire had every right to be mad.

I felt ashamed that I brought my dad, his faulty genetics, and his philandering ways into our sacred marriage.

Claire would never judge. I don't know what I was thinking—or not thinking.

Then I thought about her selling and taking Adderall, and I knew in my heart she would never start this mess intentionally. Why was I being so hard on her? It was nothing to just blow off, of course, but I hadn't offered any comfort and I wasn't sure why.

Was I taking my anger about the Li-Fraumeni Syndrome out on Claire? She was on my side. My head started to hurt thinking about all of this.

I went inside and grabbed a second cup of coffee and waited for Loretta to arrive. I thought I would FaceTime with Drew before she came.

Drew

My phone rang, and it was my dad from Canada on FaceTime. I picked up, happy to see his face. He said he was just calling to check in and see how mom and I were doing. I told him that mom and I had gone out to dinner, and she was acting like she used too. He seemed really glad to hear it.

He told me about his half-sisters and how great it was to meet them. He also told me that Jean wasn't feeling very well, and his timing was very good for the visit. He asked if I had been able to sleep and how I was coping with waiting for the test results. I let him know that I had been spending a lot of time with Lainey and it was helping.

We talked about baseball and school, and I asked him how he was feeling. He assured me that he was feeling fine and reminded me that his scans were clear. We said good night and promised to talk again in a couple of days.

Gary

It was now day 10 of the visit. Loretta arrived, and Bill went to get Jean. A few minutes later he came back and told us she needed more rest.

That was concerning, but she had been doing her best every day to show me around and fill me in on our history.

Loretta and I decided to spend the day together and let Jean rest. Loretta and her husband had two kids, a boy and a girl. They were both in their 20s. Her daughter was an RN, and her son was a journalist. Both of them were married with good partners.

I asked her about Jean, and she admitted she was having a lot of bad days. She explained that Jean had breast cancer five years ago, which was when they found out about the Li-Fraumeni Syndrome, so once she was finished with her treatments they checked her every year with an MRI and other tests for any other flare-ups. Then two years ago they found a smooth muscle tumor, Leiomyosarcoma. They took it out in December two years ago. They had hoped they had seen the last of it, and then seven months ago came this.

Loretta told me that Jean was in surgery for over six hours, and they had to remove her spleen (which is your immune system), then they took out part of her pancreas to get a very tiny tumor. They thought they had gotten it all but at her seven-month checkup they found it had spread. They said most cancers showed up early, but our dad was in his 50s and Jean was close to 50 when she found the breast cancer. The statistics said a woman with Li-Fraumeni Syndrome has a 90 percent chance of cancer by 60 years of age.

She told me that she follows a group for Li-Fraumeni Syndrome families, and one family said their grandfather had it and he was in his 80s but had never had cancer.

That made me happy to hear. I asked her if she was tested. She said she was, but thankfully she didn't have it. I wondered what she thought about Jean's kids not being tested.

She said she thought it was better to know what you were up against.

She told me about the Toronto protocol, which most Li-Fraumeni Syndrome patients followed. It recommended MRIs and other yearly and quarterly tests. Toronto SickKids Hospital did a study on kids with the gene and monitored one group following a protocol and another group that did not. After five years, there was a big difference. The kids they were just watching, not following the protocol, had so many deaths comparatively speaking that now all Li-Fraumeni Syndrome patients worldwide follow it.

I asked her if there was anything we could buy for Jean, and she said the most important thing was being there for her. Jean was so happy to meet me and learn about my beautiful family. A lot of her friends had stopped checking in. She was sure they felt like they didn't know what to say, but the reaching out had meant everything to her.

I told her I could only imagine how difficult this was for her as well, as the two sisters seemed as thick as thieves. Loretta said she couldn't imagine life without Jean, adding that she thought they would be little old ladies going to yard sales and sitting on the porch drinking tea and gossiping.

I asked her if she could tell me more about Jean since I felt like my opportunity to get to know her better was slipping away.

She said she had called her "J" since the time they were teenagers. "J" was always a bookworm. While Loretta was outside playing, Jean would be inside reading the classics like "Little Women," "Alice In Wonderland," "The Swiss Family Robinson," books by Hans Christian Andersen, and the Nancy Drew and Hardy Boys series.

"I could go on," Loretta told me. "Jean's nose was always in a book. Although she did spend some time outside playing, she was fair-skinned and auburn-haired so she tended to burn. She had a fear of heights and tight spaces, and she couldn't put her head underwater. So as kids we loved the beach, but she wouldn't jump off the raft or swim underwater. Once at our grandparents a group of the cousins talked her into going into the hayloft, which required you to climb up the ladder on the side of the barn and then step off into the hayloft, but to get down you had to swing back out onto the ladder. She couldn't do it. No matter how much we tried she couldn't get down, so we had to get Uncle Gerald, one of my mom's older brothers, who lived just across the field to come down and he had to go into the hayloft and move a lot of bales of hay and open the trapdoor in the floor and lower her down."

Loretta was smiling while reminiscing, I had a visual of Jean in her youth.

"J was very smart, just like our dad," Loretta continued. "One of dad's aunts told me once that dad finished grade school early because they bumped him ahead and he was done with grade 8 by the age of 12, but the high school had a rule that you had to be 13 to go, so he stayed home for a year until he was 13. Here is a funny story that I never knew until recently. J failed grade 8 and I could never understand that since she was so smart, and then I reached out to one of her best friends to update her on Jean's condition, and she told me that it was on purpose. Her friend Cathy said that she and their other friend Jo-Anne were a year behind Jean and they always hung out together, so they made a pact that J would fail grade 8 so they could all go to high school together, and that is just what she did."

That was J, loyal to a fault.

It was easier to come to grips with something like this when someone was old and had had a good long life. She was too young.

I agreed and expressed how happy I was to be there and meet both of them. Although we had just met, I felt like I had known them both for so long.

We went back to the house and Jean was still sleeping. Bill called the doctor, who planned to come by in the morning.

Bill, Loretta and I had dinner and sat around and talked. At about 8 p.m., I peeked into Jean's room, and she invited me in.

She was so tired. She asked me to sit down and started to talk to me, almost in a whisper.

"I am so glad that I found you, and learned about Claire and Drew," she said. "It has really brought me happiness to know you. Gary, don't hold a grudge against Claire, she made some mistakes. If Li-Fraumeni Syndrome has taught me anything, it's that life is so short. We waste so much energy on stupid things. To find someone that you are able to be vulnerable with, laugh and cry with, share children with is a gift. Don't be stubborn and throw that away to prove a point."

I wanted to call Claire and tell her I was so sorry for not letting her in and also for not being as supportive as I could have been with her battle with Adderall. I didn't want us to break up, I wanted to stay. I wanted to work on things.

Claire

It had been 10 days since Gary had left for his trip, and I missed him. Who knew I would crave the noise I had once complained about? As I was doing the dishes, my phone rang. Speak of the devil.

Gary was FaceTiming.

Of course, I looked my absolute worst. My hair was up in a bun, I had no makeup on, and I never knew how to hold the phone so that I didn't look like I had three chins. I couldn't do anything about it, so I answered before I missed the call.

I asked him how the trip was and he said it was wonderful getting to know his family but he didn't think that Jean had much longer.

She wasn't responding to chemo, and she had spent the last two days in bed, he told me. The doctor had come by yesterday and Jean decided that she wanted to stop treatment and not ruin the little time she had left.

My heart sank for Jean, but also for Gary. He had been looking for this connection his whole life, and how sad it was to find it and have it snatched away within months.

"Gary, I am so sorry to hear that," I said as he began crying.

"Claire, I am so sorry I didn't allow you to come with me," he said. "I don't know what I was thinking. That is just it, I wasn't thinking. I have been such a dick, and I wish I could take it back.

I wish you had come with me to the doctor, and I wish you were here with me now. I was a jerk when you were explaining that you had a problem with the Adderall. I was hurt that you didn't tell me you were struggling, but I did the same thing to you. I really have no excuse, but I want to try and fix this if you do."

Words I had been waiting to hear.

I felt cautious, but hopeful.

"Gary, I have longed to hear you say that. I am sorry about what you are going through now, but we are going to have to see what happens when you get home.

As much as I want to pretend that none of this ever happened, you weren't there for me. I know you were going through your own shit, I get that, but I really felt abandoned, and I don't have that same level of trust that I used to."

As I said the words, part of me wanted to just shout out, "OK, let's get back together." But if there is one thing I am learning in therapy is that you have to deal with your problems, not swallow them.

I didn't realize how Gary's reaction to my Adderall issue hurt me, but he didn't have my back.

"I am open to trying," I told him, "but why don't you focus on your sisters and we can discuss this more when you come home?"

"Can I come home," he asked, " or do I go home to that crappy apartment?"

I wanted him to come home, but I said since it was a month-to-month lease I thought he should go back to his apartment. And then we should date.

I could see on his face he was disappointed, but I didn't completely shut him down so he said that was fair.

He was coming home in a week, and we still had to get Drew's results.

We hung up and I felt more hopeful than I had in months.

Gary

I just FaceTimed Claire, and I thought she would be thrilled that I wanted to come home, but I had really hurt her. We were now going to "date."

I was happy that not all hope was lost, but I guess it wasn't the reaction I was expecting. I had to focus on Jean now since she was fading fast, and I had a lifetime of missed memories to catch up on.

She had been moved to the local hospital. She was bedridden, and Lorretta and I took turns giving her ice chips and just sitting with her.

There were times that she did perk up and had enough energy to talk, but most of the time she was just sleeping.

Bill was beside himself. They had been married for 46 years. The only reason he wasn't completely losing it was because watching her suffer was more painful than contemplating her not being here.

Bill and I talked a lot about how the cancer had impacted their relationship. Interestingly enough, it wasn't in the ways I suspected.

"In some ways it has brought us closer together," he told me.

"When you have cancer as aggressive as Jean's it makes you vulnerable. She had to let me bathe her and clean up her throw-up and allow me into her battle. That is another level of intimacy. Although not the most pleasant, we are a cohesive unit, fighting together. I think what we both realized is that life is so fleeting so when she is having a good day we don't want to waste it. We thoroughly enjoy the smallest things we are able to still do together. We no longer fight over money or the stupid things that used to bother us. We cherish the friendship and love that we have enjoyed for 48 years. We reminisce and remind each other how lucky we are to have an everlasting love.

She no longer yells at me for not putting the cap on the toothpaste. It all seems so irrelevant now. I don't regret our arguments, that is just how life goes when you are together for so long, but she is the love of my life, and I am going to spend these last days making sure there is no doubt in her mind that she was my person."

Bill's words resonated with me.

I thanked Bill for sharing his insight, and we went to check on Jean. She couldn't really drink but was subsisting on ice chips. She was now sleeping 22 out of 24 hours a day. Sometimes she seemed like she was seeing things and was smiling but yet she wasn't really conscious. Her vital signs were all over the place. The doctor had had us move Jean to the hospital so he could monitor her more frequently. Her blood pressure was often very low. Her pulse was thready and fast. The doctor explained the autonomic nervous system was shutting down and she was also dehydrated.

She was also mottling. This is often a sign of impending death. Apparently, he explained it happens when peripheral circulation, especially in capillaries, is poor. Blood flow tends to slow down and causes purplish or reddish patches on the lower extremities.

Loretta, Bill and I sat around her bed for most of the day. I had been messaging with Henri a few times, and he wanted us to FaceTime so he could be with us too as she crossed over.

I dialed him since it seemed like the end was imminent and he picked up as if he were waiting by the phone.

We each took a moment to tell Jean that we loved her, and then after Henri shared his sentiments, Loretta and I left the room for Bill to say goodbye to his bride.

Gary

The mood in the house was somber. I called Claire and told her of Jean's passing and asked her for a status on Drew's test results. She said she would call the doctor to see when the results would be in.

Normally, I would have been crawling out of my skin to get them, but now I was hoping for a slight delay so I could be here for Jean's services.

I told Claire that it was peaceful and that we were all in the room, even Henri over FaceTime.

We talked a bit about Loretta, and how close they were, and how I imagined how hard this would be for her.

I told Claire that I wished she was with me, and she said she did too. We continued to talk, and she told me she would text me when she heard back from the doctor about the timing of Drew's results.

Jean's arrangements were made for the most part in advance since her death wasn't a surprise. My hope was that I would be able to attend the funeral.

I wouldn't let it be known that I was in fact her half-brother. I would just introduce myself as a friend of the family. I didn't want the attention, nor did I want to recount my story and deflect the attention away from Jean, who deserved to be honored.

Claire texted me back and let me know that the lab was running a few days behind, and I had until Wednesday of next week to get home.

I thanked her and let the family know that I would stay to pay my respects to Jean and help out in whatever way I could.

It was weird that I felt so close to this family that I had known so briefly. Blood really is thicker than water, at least in this case. Perhaps it was because I had longed for this family my whole life.

I thought about my son and how I cherished our relationship. From the moment I cut that cord, I knew there would be nothing I wouldn't do for him. As time went on, that feeling only grew stronger. There is a special bond between a parent and a child that is the most powerful connection. I questioned how my biological parents chose to give that up and my adoptive parents didn't cherish it. I would never take Drew for granted. He was something we got right.

The service was beautiful. It was no surprise that the church was filled. Jean had a number of friends, and relatives came from near and far to say goodbye and to comfort the family.

I longed for my Claire to be at my side. I reminded myself that I didn't invite her, so it was my own fault that I was there alone.

After a very long day we all ended up back at Jean and Bill's house, sitting around the table. Bill and Loretta shared some funny Jean stories and talked about how feisty and full of life she was. I was happy to learn that although definitely cut too short, her life was well spent.

I packed up my stuff and got ready to head back home. The time in Canada has been cathartic, and I would always be grateful that I came. I promised Bill and Loretta that I would stay in touch, and I was sincere.

Now I was anxious to see my wife and son. I wasn't looking forward to the doctor's visit where we would learn what Drew was in store for. As I started the journey back, I left the radio off. I was going to take the drive to think long and hard about how I wanted to handle my life going forward. Some of what would happen was up to me.

I couldn't believe I was going back to that crappy apartment. Well, I should believe it, it was my own doing. I'd really made some stupid decisions of late, and I had to start thinking before I acted. The apartment was cleaner than one might imagine, but it was sparse and lonely. I missed my family.

I wanted to message with Henri, who had taken Jean's death particularly hard.

I typed my usual "Hey Bro, you there?"

"Bro, I am here."

I asked him how he was holding up.

"Tough times, bro, for everybody. I knew she, do you say 'deteriorate?' But it happened so fast. I feel a deep malaise."

I thought about it—Henri and Jean had been talking for years now. They were very close.

He also hadn't been tested.

"Henri, it might be too soon for me to bring this up, but you are my brother, so I am. Did you take the test yet?"

"I did go for the screening, mostly for my daughter, but remember, we have socialized medicine here. I will be waiting for months."

That was so unfair. I knew how long three weeks felt. I told him I was happy he did the screening, and I was sorry for the wait.

He told me he had written a poem for Jean. It was written it in French, but I saw it in English thanks to Google.

For the tears to come
There will be light
That could not be blown
Nor by any wind
Nor by any night
It is a candle
Lit up in my Heart
That could not be dimmed
Nor by any wind
Nor by any night
It's your gentleness
You give all around

That could not be stopped
Nor by any wind
Nor by any night
It'll live forever
In hearts you gather
That nothing could felt
Nor by any wind
Nor by any night
For the years to come
There will be a soul
That could not be blown
Nor by any wind
Nor by any night

I wish I could have heard him recite it in French, but the pain and sentiment in his words translated.

His heart was broken.

I told him it was beautiful and that I knew Jean was smiling from heaven. Henri had the gentlest heart, and I was so happy he was my brother.

I reminded him that we were getting Drew's test results tomorrow and he said he would be praying for us.

We said our goodnights and I promised to fill him in, no matter if the news was good or bad.

I closed by saying, "I love you, bro, and I am so happy to have you in my life."

"Gary, the feeling is mutual."

I tried my best to close my eyes, but when I did I flashed back to my trip and felt such a hole in my heart. I have had many longer relationships that have ended, and I couldn't have cared less.

The intensity and connection I felt with Jean was deep. I would miss our talks. Then I thought of poor Bill and Loretta. I couldn't imagine how they would move on, but they would. This was the cruel part of life.

What was that saying? *Better to have loved and lost than never to have loved.* I guess I agreed with Tennyson, but the pain was palpable.

I must have drifted off to sleep, which I desperately needed. It was after 9 a.m. when I awoke, and I had to go pick up Claire and Drew. I hopped in the shower and grabbed some coffee. I thought and said the words out loud, "Jean, if you can do anything from up there, please spare my son."

Claire

Gary should be home any minute, or I should say home to his apartment. We had never been separated for this long. I did miss him. I was going to tell him to just come to our house, but then I decided against it. I wasn't trying to play games, but he had really hurt me. I needed him to think long and hard about what he did or didn't do. I had really needed him, and he wasn't there.

If he came home, we would have to agree to no more secrets. I thought we would have to go back to Saturday night dates. This didn't mean expensive dinners or even going out, but rather talking. We somehow had started taking each other for granted and stopped communicating.

He had had a long drive and an emotional visit, but hopefully he had gotten some sleep. We were meeting up to get Drew's results the following day.

Who was I kidding? No one would be sleeping.

Drew asked us if Lainey could come with us to his appointment, and I said no. I felt terrible, but I thought it should just be us.

I wondered if that was a mistake. I knew Lainey provided him comfort, but I wasn't sure what the results would be and they had only been dating for a short time. I thought it should just be the three of us.

Gary FaceTimed when he got home. I was relieved he was back in the country and wished he were here so we could talk about tomorrow, but as my son told me, there was no use worrying before we knew if there was anything to worry about. To waste time speculating would only make my anxiety worse.

Gary would be over to the house soon enough, and we would drive into the city for our 1 p.m. appointment. I was sure no one would want to have lunch or talk beforehand.

As I predicted, my night was spent tossing and turning, and I thought I heard Drew on his video game. I didn't see a point in telling him to shut it down. It might be the longest night of our lives.

Finally, the sun was coming up and I put on a big pot of coffee. I got on the Peloton to kill an hour, and then hopped in the shower.

Now it was 8 a.m. I felt like I was going to crawl out of my skin. Drew came down and I asked him if he wanted something to eat.

He declined and said his stomach was too nervous. I asked him if he wanted to talk. Surprisingly, he said yes.

"What if I have it?" he asked. "I'm really scared."

I hugged him and said I was scared too. I let him know that if we were diligent with the screenings if he had the gene there was a good likelihood that we could stay in front of it.

"This sucks," he said.

I said it sure did.

Gary walked in, and we hugged. If felt nice to be in his arms. He then hugged Drew and we got into the car.

There was so much to talk about, but no one said a word. I looked at my boy and thought it was so unfair that he was being forced into adulthood prematurely due to these unforeseen circumstances. It would be impossible to regain that carefree feeling of childhood after experiencing the threat of cancer and the possibility of your family breaking up.

I looked at my husband and felt sad thinking about his upbringing and his insecurities around being adopted and unwanted. I thought about his biological father and felt pity and anger for a man I had never met and would never know.

We were running into traffic, but we had left so early it was fine.

We finally arrived at the doctor's office, and Gary and I sat. Drew was pacing up and down the hall until we were finally called in.

The doctor asked us to all take a seat.

He cut right to the chase and said he had some really good news: Drew had tested negative for the mutation. I burst into tears. I don't think I have ever felt such relief in my life. Oh, thank God. I looked over and Gary and Drew were crying too.

Finally, some good news.

Drew

I heard the words, and I wanted someone to pinch me. I felt like I had been holding my breath for three weeks. My parents were both crying, and I realized I was too. I asked my mom if I could go and call Lainey, and she said of course.

I called her and she picked up on the first ring. I told her I didn't have the gene and she was the first person I wanted to tell.

She told me how relieved she was, and we professed our love to one another and hung up. I went back to find my parents.

We were all grinning like idiots, but the news meant I could be a normal kid once again. On the car ride home, I told my parents that I had been doing a lot of thinking, and now that I would be able to make plans for a future. I decided that I wanted to pursue a degree in medicine, focused on researching cancer and other rare diseases.

My mom said it was very noble but it was a huge undertaking. Was I sure?

I replied that I wasn't sure but I felt compelled to see if I could make an impact in the fight against cancer.

It wasn't something that I had ever spent any time thinking about, but now I doubted it would ever be far from the recesses of my mind.

I would be applying for college in the fall and up until this point, there had been nothing of interest that I'd wanted to pursue. Suddenly, it seemed crystal clear.

I thought about the fact that Li-Fraumeni Syndrome was something I had never even heard of. It made me realize how many diseases were out there that needed attention. I had always wanted to do something with a purpose, and this hit so close to home I felt like it was a calling.

I was then reminded that just because I was out of the woods, my father wasn't.

"Dad, I am so sorry to be celebrating while you still have to contend with Li-Fraumeni."

"Drew, although there wouldn't have been anything I could have done to prevent it, I would have felt so guilty if I had passed this down to you. You have every right to celebrate, and I am equally ecstatic. You are an extension of me, and the relief I feel is hard to explain, but I bet you can imagine."

" I have to ask you guys something."

"Shoot."

" I would like us to have dinner at our house tonight as a family."

My dad said that was entirely up to my mother. I waited for her to chime in.

Claire

I was so happy Drew had suggested a family dinner so I didn't have to. This was the happiest I had felt in forever. If there was ever something to make you appreciate what was really important in life, it was a clean bill of health. My baby was OK.

I loved how he told Gary and I that he was contemplating going to college to become a doctor and doing something meaningful.

I too had been thinking about a change. While I have loved my career, I wasn't getting the fulfillment I needed to make me feel like I have left my footprint on this world. Depending on how things went with Gary and our relationship, I was contemplating going back to school to become either an addiction counselor or a therapist. Since I had been going to Reclaim You, I felt like a new person. I have hope, I have understanding around some of my idiosyncrasies but, most importantly, I have learned to accept and appreciate all of the things that make me me. Without someone guiding me through some deep introspection, I don't think I would have dug myself out of the dark hole I was in.

I think everyone could use a little therapy. I was considering suggesting that Gary get his own therapist to deal with his adoption, the loss of his sister, our marriage. Who couldn't use a bit of objective feedback?

I knew my boss Jeff would be disappointed if I left and money would be tight, but I was a firm believer in paying it forward.

I wondered if I could do the schooling at night. Maybe I could take some Adderall to keep me focused. Kidding.

Dinner was perfect. I loved the dynamic of the three of us together. We were all in good moods, and it was evident that the cloud had been lifted, at least a little.

Of course, we still had to deal with Gary's diagnosis and the fact that our marriage was far from stable. But at this very moment, all felt right with the world.

At the end of the night, Drew went off to text Lainey, and I felt like I was on a first date.

I told Gary I was so happy he was home and that I really enjoyed our evening. He said that he didn't have to go. I told him he did.

As much as I wanted him to stay, and as happy as I was to see him, we had some work to do. We both had made some huge mistakes and had done things that we both won't forget.

He said he understood, but he really wanted to stay. He told me that I looked really good.

There was a stirring in my loins, and although I was tired and hated leaving dishes in the sink, I wanted to see if my lubes and vegetables had made any difference.

I said I guessed he could stay for some dessert. He looked elated. I knew this wasn't the way to solve our problems, but against my better judgement I invited him upstairs.

His touch felt electrifying. I tried not to let the worry of not being able to climax ruin the moment. It was hard to get out of my own head, but I tried and concentrated on what was happening.

We had sex, and I have to say it, those smoothies are useless and empty calories. Of course, I faked it again and he looked like the cat that swallowed the canary. I now wanted him to leave so I could grab my vibrator. This was a serious damn problem.

I was sure now that it had nothing to do with Gary, and everything to do with my age. I didn't want to spoil the mood, so we lay in each other's arms until I told him I thought it was time he left.

He wanted to stay but I told him I wanted to work on us. This was nice, I said, but it didn't change things. You need to date me, I told him.

I also planned on talking to my therapist about how to tell Gary that I was still having issues. Not only did I feel inadequate, but I felt too young to be done with my sex life. I didn't understand what was going on. I had been off the Adderall for months now. It was really depressing and embarrassing.

Gary

I couldn't believe Claire was making me go home in the middle of the night. I mean, we have lived together for decades. I am old and tired, why couldn't I just stay? I got it, and I sort of had done this to myself, but it seemed rather foolish to kick me out now. It took me back to when we were dating, and I was waiting to be invited in for the night. Full circle, I guess.

I reflected on what an amazing day this had been. My son didn't have the gene. Everything else that had seemed so paramount was now insignificant.

My family is everything. I had to make a concerted effort to get our relationship back on track. Claire had been very supportive about the trip to Canada and her devotion to our son was unwavering. She also hadn't thrown the fact that I had kept my diagnosis from her in my face.

It seemed unfair to hold a grudge when I was far from perfect. But it felt like my old Claire was back. The one I wanted to spend my life with.

I decided not to argue and to go home and relish in my afterglow. Glad to know our sex life was in fact OK. That had always been a constant for us. I wondered how it would be after such a long time. Thankfully some things never change.

Claire

I couldn't wait to get to Reclaim You and have my one-on-one therapy session. I felt a bit unhinged after all of yesterday's events.

Drew's news was amazing, but I really didn't follow the steps of my program by having sex with Gary.

I should have insisted he left after dinner, reminding him that we had work to do.

I was almost afraid to tell the therapist, but I wanted to understand why I was so impulsive. I also wanted to ask her if I should go into more detail with Gary about my physical issues. How intercourse was a bit painful and not what it once was.

I thought coming off the Adderall would have made a big difference, but that wasn't the case.

This was going to add a layer of complexity to the issues that Gary and I already had to address.

I sat down with her and blurted out that Drew didn't have the gene. She was genuinely thrilled for me.

This reminded me why I loved coming here. My therapist was so sincere and invested in my success.

I then told her at the request of Drew we all had had a family dinner, which we hadn't done in close to a year.

She asked me how that made me feel. My initial reaction was "thrilled." It felt like I was getting my old life back.

She then said if your old life was good, why do you think you started taking Adderall? This was a great question, but it made me mad.

I said I had told her I was feeling invisible and trapped. She asked me what has changed since that time, pointing out that Drew was more independent and would be going off to college, I had the same job, but Gary still didn't share his health scare with me until after he had gotten the diagnosis.

I asked her why she was trying to make me feel badly and she replied that she was trying to make sure I saw that things could very easily fall right back to where they were if I didn't make some changes.

Drew's good news had made everyone euphoric but at the end of the day, I needed to work on my communication with Gary. That didn't mean sexual communication, she said. It meant "use your words."

Reclaim You recommends people not get involved in a relationship or make any major changes until they had been in the program for at least a year, she said. She added that she thought I was making tremendous progress, but that I had a long way to go.

I thought about her words.

I told her I was really scared that in addition to our communication issues I was going to now have to deal with the sexual issues I was having. What if Gary didn't think it was worth trying to fix?

She posed this question.

"Would you give up on him if he couldn't get an erection? If that hasn't been an issue yet, it could become one in the future. Would you give up on him?

You discuss it, you don't fake it, and you see if you can find other ways that may alleviate your issues. If you are worried about this while you are in the act there is no way you will be able to let go and release.

Just something to consider. We are out of time today, but I hope you know I am on your side. There is no shortcut if this process is going to work. You have to do the steps."

That certainly brought my mood down, but I knew she was right, and this discussion with Gary would have to happen sooner rather than later. I needed to know if he was willing to add this to our pile of problems that needed attention.

I decided to take the first step and see if Gary wanted to take a walk on the beach and just talk.

I was going to remind him that we couldn't fix this by taking one walk, but we had to start somewhere.

I called him up and made the ask, and he said it sounded like a great idea. I wasn't sure if I was going to bring up sex during our first conversation, but I thought we had made a mistake getting physical so quickly. My therapist had made some good points, and I didn't want to fall back into old habits. One day at a time.

Gary

I was working on a big project at work, which was allowing me to throw myself into crunching numbers rather than thinking about the whirlwind that was my life. It felt nice to just do something normal and unemotional. In accounting, once things balance, you're done and you can move on, unlike emotional situations, which need constant attention. There was a reason I had chosen a profession with tangible finite outcomes.

Claire invited me on a walk, and I was genuinely looking forward to it. Aside from Jean and my chats with Henri, I didn't really have a friend to talk to. I had missed our conversations.

Saturday turned out to be a sunny day, and I saw her in the distance. She was a beautiful woman, and I was so happy to be there.

We said our hellos and I began.

"Claire, I owe you an apology. I never realized how being adopted has impacted my life. I have never had a sense of belonging. Don't get me wrong, when I married you and we had Drew, I felt I had my own family. You have given that to me, but prior to that, I was sort of on my own. I have felt so detached for so long, and then I met my sisters and Henri, and I felt like I too had roots. I never dreamed that there would be a medical condition to consider. I just pictured a happy family reunion like on TV.

The diagnosis pulled the rug right out from under me. I have been emotionally up and down like a yo-yo. I didn't purposely exclude you, but I was barely able to make sense of things for myself, let alone share.

I said I did it to shield you, but I think I thought if I didn't speak about it, it wasn't real. The hill looked insurmountable, and I truly just didn't want to consider that I could have this gene, and this syndrome.

In retrospect, history tells me that anything you are involved in always works out better. I am infinitely sorry.

I also apologize for not recognizing that you were struggling. You always have everything under control, so I think I just took it for granted that you are always fine. There were probably signs that I wasn't looking for because I was submerged in my own shit.

I wish you would have come to me, but I know you could say the same thing. I am hoping we can try to start leaning on each other, which we used to do so well."

Claire was quick to respond.

"Thank you, Gary, that makes a lot of sense, and I can't even imagine what must have been going on in your mind. I have always marveled at how you care for your adoptive parents, even though when it was their turn to support you, they were absent.

I tried not to show my anger for their lack of empathy because you don't hold it against them, but it is hard. I am angry that they never made you feel wanted and part of their family.

In my case, I don't think I realized that I was feeling lost until I started feeling like I wasn't really needed. Drew is a man/boy, you were distracted, my job is repetitive and boring, and I just sort of felt invisible. I was just looking for a jump-start. It was foolish to start taking pills, and then selling was just the next level. It made me feel excited and interesting, which I know isn't good. I am just being truthful.

As I continued to get in over my head, I was ashamed to come to you. It just snowballed out of control. I am sorry too."

We continued to stroll down the beach holding hands. I felt content. We decided to grab some lunch and play a round of miniature golf.

I didn't ask to go to our house and she didn't extend an invitation, but that was OK. When we parted ways, I went back to the apartment and reached out to Henri.

As soon as I messaged him, I saw the three dots. It was like he was always there for me.

"Henri, I have the best news, Drew doesn't have the gene."

"Gary, one could not hope for better news, I am so happy for you, bro. I wish I would get my results, but it looks like I have three more months to wait. How are you feeling?"

I told him I felt absolutely fine, which was scary since I knew that I wasn't. I also let him know that I had scans scheduled every three months for the rest of my life.

"That is a real drag, but I guess it is good to know so you can monitor. I am very nervous to get my results."

I told him that knowledge is power, and he had to do it for his daughter.

I then told Henri about my walk with Claire and how we were going to try and work on our communication with each other. I let him know I still thought she was my person and that if there was one thing that Jean had tried to impress upon me was that you can't sweat the small stuff. When you look at the big picture, what really matters is your tribe.

"I miss Jean, she was a beautiful soul," Henri wrote.

I let him know that although she had just come into my life, I felt a tremendous loss as well. She was so kind and insightful. I finally had this connection and then it was gone.

I started to tear up and decided to end the chat before I really started to cry.

We disconnected and I made myself a disgusting frozen dinner.

Drew

I couldn't wait to see Lainey. We had both been so concerned about my results it would be nice to go out and do something fun without a worry.

I asked her if she wanted to go to an Italian street fair in New York City and spend the entire day together. She loved the idea, and we decided to take the train in and just spend the day in the city.

They had shut down Canal and Houston streets, and there was one food vendor after the next. There were a few games, but mostly the fair was just eating and drinking.

We visited several booths until we couldn't eat another bite. We decided to walk around the village and find some vintage record shops and random bookstores.

We stopped into a Starbucks so we could use the restrooms before we continued exploring the city. The day was amazing, and I felt so happy. We had been strolling around for hours and we both started to yawn a little and I suggested we head back home.

We held hands as we walked to the train. On the train Lainey put her head on my shoulder. It felt so natural, and I told her that this had been a perfect day.

"Drew, it was almost perfect, but I have to tell you something."

I panicked, praying she wasn't going to dump me.

"I made myself throw up in Starbucks. Street festivals are really hard for me because there is so much food, I eat too much, and then I need to get rid of it because I feel so guilty.

I am so embarrassed, but I think I need help."

I asked her if she would mind if I spoke to my mom about it. My mother gave really solid advice, and I trusted her to keep whatever I shared with her in confidence.

Lainey hesitated and said she felt weird about me telling her but knew she needed the help.

As we pulled up to the station, I looked her in the eyes and assured her that I wasn't going anywhere. I was there for her, and she hugged me.

I walked her home and planned to ask my mom what the heck I could do to help her.

I was grateful that my old mom seemed to be back. I would ask her in the morning.

Claire

I so enjoyed my time with Gary. I had no idea he had all of that going on in his mind. I was sure Ancestry had triggered a lot of those buried emotions. I was doing my best not to let him see how concerned I was about the Li-Fraumeni Syndrome.

No one really knew how long they had on this earth but knowing that you didn't have the gene that suppressed cancer made your mortality top of mind.

I decided the next time we met I was going to tell Gary that part of my sobriety was to abstain from sex for a full year in treatment.

This would take the pressure off me so that I could concentrate on working the steps, and I could do some work with my therapist and perhaps my gynecologist to see if there was anything I could do.

It sounds like I was obsessed with sex, which I wasn't. I always enjoyed it but, truthfully, it was more the feeling of intimacy and connection that I was afraid of losing. Not the actual act.

I guess I had watched too many Lifetime movies and I saw couples well into their 70s having sex without any issues. Now when I consulted with my doctors and other friends, it seemed that women dry up and stop producing estrogen, which is sort of needed when it comes to arousal.

At the end of the day, I just wanted to feel that special connection we had always shared. Sometimes I simply wanted him to grab my hand or play with my hair.

I was such a perfectionist that I felt like my body was failing me despite the fact that it did give me a beautiful son. If I thought about the aging process, I wasn't in the fertility phase of life, so it made sense.

It also made me feel old, which in itself was depressing.

We were aging together, so rather than keep this inside, I felt like I should just tell him how inadequate I was feeling and see if he had similar concerns.

If I knew he was worried about his own performance or moving through yet another phase of life, I would feel more secure because we could face our fears together.

While I didn't want to blurt it out as we are just starting to really talk, I felt like if I shared this huge weight that was on my mind, perhaps I could relax a little and let the process work as it was meant to.

I was going to ask my therapist if she felt I should bring this up. I didn't know how I had ever lived without her. She was my sounding board. When she affirmed my feelings, I started to trust my own instincts. I hadn't been able to do that in quite some time.

So I went into my session, and she asked me what had been going on. I told her about our walk, the lunch, and our conversation. She told me that it was fantastic and exactly what I should be doing. Communicating.

I told her that I would like to explain to Gary that I'm not supposed to make any major changes and I am supposed to abstain from sex for a year. I asked her if it was too soon for me to bring this up.

She reminded me that there was no prescribed timeline for our conversations, but she also acknowledged that this obviously had been troubling me and thought it would be good for me to get it off my chest.

She also recommended that I don't necessarily use the program as an excuse but let him know that I was feeling insecure because I was having some physical changes due to menopause.

I thought that sounded reasonable, but I dreaded it. As close as Gary and I were, we still didn't go to the bathroom with the door open or fart in front of each other. We were shy in some ways because of how we were raised. This was going to be difficult for me to bring up but if we were ever going to make progress, we had to address the uncomfortable.

When I got home, Drew was waiting for me. He asked me if we could talk. I was thrilled at the prospect.

He then told me that Lainey was making herself throw up.

Wow, that wasn't the topic I thought we would be discussing.

I said, OK, take a seat and back up.

"Was it a one-time thing? Did you guys have a fight? How did this come about?"

Drew explained that Lainey had told him when he had confided in her about the Li-Fraumeni Syndrome scare. He didn't realize she was still doing it, but he said she actually had done it when they were together on Saturday. He told me that he had asked her permission to confide in me and she agreed.

I told Drew very honestly that although bulimia wasn't my expertise, I could imagine food being somewhat like my pill addiction. I had learned at Reclaim You that most of these crutches are really a symptom of a bigger problem.

I wondered if she would be open to coming down to the center to talk to someone. I would make sure it wasn't my therapist. Or perhaps attending a meeting with the group designated for teens. This way she wouldn't feel as if I was invading her space, but at the same time she would know I was there in the periphery.

Drew thanked me and told me he would speak with Lainey. He hugged me and told me how happy he was to have me back.

Claire

I hadn't spoken to Lainey's mom since I was in the PTA, but I knew her daughter needed help and I had to put her first. I grabbed my phone and texted, Ginger, yes, her name was Ginger. I asked her if we could meet up for a coffee.

"I told you I don't partake in your activities."

"It has to do with Lainey."

"Fine, but this better not be a plot to lure me in to buy your drugs."

I really disliked this woman and understood why Lainey wanted to throw up. We agreed to meet up at 1 p.m.

I questioned my involvement. I was newly sober, and I disliked Ginger. But I felt obliged because Drew had asked, and Lainey needed help.

I understood the feelings Lainey was struggling with. I think the food was similar to the Adderall. If I was able to help her from my experience, it would make me feel like I hadn't just wasted a year of my life.

Next, I grabbed my iPad determined to find some information that would help me contend with my menopausal symptoms. Of course, a million solutions came up with convincing testimonials, but I already had a drawer full of products, massagers and lubes that didn't seem to make any difference. I decided I was going to call for a consultation with a sex therapist. I also had better clear my cache—my search of late had been, sex, bulimia, drugs and adoption.

I hesitated for a minute but there was an actual practice to deal with these issues, so I knew it wasn't just me.

I dialed the number and got a lovely woman named Debbie. She asked me what seemed to be the problem.

I wanted to say ,"Isn't it obvious? Your center is called 'Sexual Healing.'"

Instead, I said, "I am a 53-year-old woman and have been having some issues lately, and I am hoping there is something that can be done to restore my lady parts."

"Of course," she said. She had a few questions before we got started.

OK, I said, fire away.

"Does this problem bother your partner?"

"I have been faking it, so he doesn't know there is a problem."

"Do you still have desire but just can't get aroused?"

"Yes, I would say that is accurate."

" I understand this is hard to talk about, but we like to classify sexual problems into four phases: desire, arousal, orgasm and resolution. So since I see that you are still interested in sex but are having physical issues, I feel like we can help you out. Would you like to schedule an appointment?"

I really wanted to decline, but I also wanted to fix this if I could, so I said yes. And we scheduled a consultation for Thursday at 2 p.m.

Why had I not known that this happened? No one talked about it.

Enough sex talk for the day. I hopped in the shower and prepared to meet Ginger. Yay, on to bulimia.

Drew

I let Lainey know that my mom was going to reach out to hers since she was a minor and we would need her mother's consent if she was going to intervene. Especially if her mother allowed her to go with mine to Reclaim You. Lainey said it was sad that she had her own mother but felt more comfortable talking to mine. Was that weird?

I assured her it wasn't weird at all, and I reminded her that my mom was dealing with a struggle that was similar to hers so it made total sense for her to talk with my mom.

Lainey thanked me, saying she thought this was going to be too heavy for me to deal with. I reminded her what I had just gone through and said I thought that this was how this relationship thing worked. We helped each other.

Lainey was sure that her mother was going to be resistant to admitting that her daughter was flawed. I told her to let my mother try—she was very persuasive.

We did our homework and decided to go to the mall to walk around. I was driving a lot with my dad but still not allowed to drive on my own. Why didn't I do this earlier?

I should be able to take my road test in a couple of months. Until then, I was dependent on other people for transportation.

My mom dropped us at the mall on her way to meet Lainey's mom. I normally hated shopping, but somehow when I was with Lainey it was fun.

She tried to help me with my wardrobe, another thing I never paid attention to. I guess my shorts and T-shirts could use an upgrade. We walked around for a bit, we both bought some clothes, and I asked her if she would like to grab some food. I said I hoped it was OK to suggest eating. She explained to me that it was. She said it wasn't eating at mealtime that triggered her, it was more likely to happen if she was starving and binged or if her mom criticized her. Unfortunately, she said, her mom was always on her case about something she could do better.

"When I stick to my routine, I am usually OK," she told me, "but I do appreciate you asking.

My dentist actually would have ratted me out if your mom didn't. Apparently, the acid from your stomach erodes the enamel on your teeth. He told me that I have to stop purging or I am in for a bunch of root canals. Another motivating bit of information to encourage me to get a handle on it.

I feel so awful that I am doing this to myself, but somehow, I can't stop. He was going to tell her, but I asked him to give me a week and that I would prefer to do it myself."

I wasn't really sure how to respond, but I assured her I thought she would be able to get it under control with the support of my mother and Reclaim You.

Claire

I dropped the kids off at the mall and continued on to meet Ginger. This should be really interesting. We decided to meet at the Starbucks in town. As soon as I got out of the car, I spotted her wearing her Lululemon leggings and sports bra. I bet she doesn't even work out. Her hair and makeup were perfect, and she was sporting a Louis Vuitton tote that cost more than my entire outfit.

I, on the other hand, didn't have makeup on but was wearing a super cute dress, with sandals and a fresh pedi. I knew who I was dealing with.

We ordered our skinny vanilla lattes and sat down. She was looking me up and down, and I started.

"Look Ginger, I am sorry about the whole PTA situation, but I am here because I have grown really fond of Lainey since she started dating Drew, and I am concerned about her."

"Why are you concerned about Lainey?"

I asked her if she knew that Lainey was binging and purging. She told me that was simply ridiculous. She would know if that was going on.

I let her know that Lainey had confided in Drew and asked for help.

"Why wouldn't she have come to me?" she asked.

As much as I wanted to tell her, "It's because you are a bitch," I told her that I thought she didn't want to disappoint her.

She considered this and softened her reply.

"I had no idea she was doing this. I did tell her she looked like she had put on a few pounds since she started dating Drew," she said.

It was hard for me to hold back at this point, but I did. I suggested to Ginger that she think very carefully about what she said to Lainey, reminding her how hard girls were on themselves at this age.

"I only told her because it is much easier to keep the weight off when you are young."

I mentioned that the kids are under so much pressure with their extracurricular activities, grades, and college prep, that it could feel a little overwhelming.

"The more Lainey knows about what she is in for, the better. She has had it pretty easy."

"Ginger, you are constantly criticizing her so of course she is going to feel insecure. No one measures up to your impossible standards. That is far from easy."

She began to get up and I stopped her.

"Look, I have been getting a lot of help from a support group that I attend at a place called Reclaim You," I said. "Would you allow me to invite Lainey to attend to see if she likes it? She is still a minor so I will need your consent, and your insurance info, but I think it could really be useful for her."

She considered it.

"If Lainey wants to go, I will get her there and supply the insurance information."

A better answer than I had hoped for.

I thanked her. I felt sorry for Lainey but was excited to tell the kids we had gotten the green light.

Gary

Claire was coming over to this shithole apartment for dinner.

I was actually attempting to cook something. There was always pizza, which we both love, if my dish didn't turn out well. I was trying to show her that I recognized all of the dinners she had cooked for me.

I was only making pasta and salad, so it was unlikely that I would screw it up, but I got some really good wine and made garlic bread to detract from the jarred tomato sauce and boring salad.

Claire arrived right on time, and I was so happy to see her. I poured us each a glass of wine. I couldn't believe I was nervous to spend the evening with my wife.

She laughed and said, "I love what you've done with the place."

"Which was absolutely nothing," I replied. "Very funny, but I don't plan on staying."

Silence.

Then she said, "Slow down, cowboy. That is the goal, but we have some work to do."

I told her I recognized that, and we took a seat on the futon. Yes, the futon.

She told me she had to tell me something that had been on her mind.

I braced myself.

"Please, whatever you need to get off your chest I would be happy to hear."

"I have been too embarrassed to go into the details, but I am still having difficulty during sex. Not only is it a little painful for me but I can't get to where I am going, if you know what I mean."

"Really? It didn't seem that way the other night."

She then told me that she had faked it because she didn't want me to think it had anything to do with me. Which did cross my mind. She said there was something going on with her body because of menopause. She said she had spoken to her doctor and also has an appointment with a sex therapist.

Generally, whenever she mentions her period, a UTI, menopause, anything to do with woman issues, I stop her midsentence, but she seemed really upset.

"I had no idea. I thought we were supposed to abstain anyway."

"Well we are, but I am really bothered by what is going on, and I am hoping there is a remedy. I hope you know that my intention is to be intimate with you again but knowing that I am having these problems is only adding to my anxiety."

"Claire, look, of course I want to have sex with you, but we're not 20-year-old kids anymore. It means something different than it used to.

I am no spring chicken either. When you offered to go with me for my screenings, not knowing if we were going to make it, I thought I was the luckiest man alive. I found a loyal sexy, smart devoted woman. That is more important to me than sex. Of course, we need to work on things so that we both find pleasure, but it's not a deal-breaker."

"That does make me feel better, but I feel so old. I never knew this was something to be worried about in my 50s. I thought we had time."

"Claire, I have a mutation on my chromosome, which is not really a selling feature, but you don't seem to be giving up on me."

I suggested we eat dinner. I have to say, Rao's sauce doesn't disappoint. That with a little Marie's Caesar dressing, wine and garlic bread, I impressed the shit out of both of us.

She told me about Ginger, Lainey, then we talked about Drew. I looked at the clock and it was midnight.

The evening had gone by in a flash, and it was wonderful.

"I'd better get going," she told me, "but I had a wonderful time."

I thanked her for coming and told her I couldn't wait for our next date.

Lainey

When I got home from the mall, my mother was waiting at the door. She almost gave me a heart attack.

"Lainey, is there something you want to talk about?"

"Not really."

" I understand you have been making yourself throw up. That is totally disgusting. Why would you be doing that?"

I immediately thought that Drew's mom hadn't done a great job of discussing my issues.

"I don't mean to do it. I just feel pressure, and it gives me a relief."

She asked me what type of pressure was compelling me to puke. I really didn't want to get into it, but I blurted out, "You just need everything to be perfect, and I can't deliver what you expect from me."

There. I had said it.

Her demeanor changed.

"Honey, I only push because I want the best for you. I want you to have every opportunity that life has to offer."

"I get that mom, but getting straight As, being 110 pounds, being on the varsity tennis team, volunteering and applying to colleges is a lot to keep up with. Sometimes, I just don't want to do it all."

"Nonsense. You love volunteering and tennis, and you said you were excited about college."

"I am, but I don't want to go to Harvard. I want to go to the University of Michigan and study social work."

"Social work? Really. Lainey, that seems like a pointless career where you won't make any money."

"Not everything is about money, mom. I want to make a difference, and I want to help other teens deal with the pressure of having a parent like you."

I stormed off and slammed the door.

After several hours of pacing in my room, I texted Drew and asked him if I could come over.

I thought you would never ask was his reply.

Drew

It was 2 a.m. and I snuck down and let Lainey in. I was pretty sure my mom would approve of me being there for her but perhaps not the letting-her-stay-in-my-room part.

She needed me so much right now, and all I wanted to do was hold her. I asked her what had happened, and she told me about her mother. That woman was such a bitch. She cut Lainey down every chance she got.

I reminded her we were months away from college, and she just had to keep her eye on the prize. She said the environment was so toxic that she didn't know how she would make it.

All of a sudden, we were kissing, and I was taking her top off. I knew this wasn't a good idea, and that wasn't my intention when I said she could come over but she was so close and I loved her so much.

I stopped and said I didn't think we should do this, she was very vulnerable, and I didn't want her to regret anything.

She told me she loved me and she was ready.

I had had no intention of having sex and I didn't have any protection. I asked her if she was on the pill, and she said she wasn't. Somehow it didn't seem to matter, and we ended up having sex. It was beautiful and I was so happy that we did—except for the part where we didn't use protection.

I considered myself pretty smart, but this was really dumb. I was praying Lainey wouldn't regret what we did, but when she stirred and her arms wrapped around me I knew she didn't.

But I was concerned that we hadn't taken any precautions and thought we should get the morning after pill just in case. When Lainey told me that you have to be 18 to get the pill and she couldn't ask her mother I knew what our only choice was. Asking my mom. I knew she would be furious, but I didn't feel like we had a choice.

When my mom woke up, I let her know that we needed to talk. She mumbled something about coffee and then saw Lainey.

We sat at the kitchen table and she asked what was going on. We recapped the fight with Lainey's mom and told her how Lainey had had to get out of the house. Then I told her that we had sex and didn't use protection.

She looked dumbfounded. I could see she was trying not to show me how disappointed she was, but she wasn't happy. And then she said she supposed we wanted her to get the morning after pill for Lainey.

My mom asked Lainey if she was prepared to tell her mother and that she didn't feel comfortable doing this behind her back.

Lainey started to cry and begged my mom to keep it between us.

Although my mother is cool, she didn't agree and said that as a parent she couldn't do that.

I was so mad at myself. I knew better.

Ginger

I couldn't believe I was being summoned to the Holden house for more lectures. Who did Claire think she was lecturing me about my daughter? The only reason I was going was because I had been dying to see the inside of their house.

Claire had already given me her opinion on how I should be raising my daughter, and I thought we'd been doing just fine without her input.

When I arrived, Lainey and Drew were there as well. I hoped I still got time to look around.

Claire invited me in, and we all made our way into the living room.

It was pretty nice inside. I was impressed.

We all sat down, and I said, "Can someone please tell me what I am doing here? I am very busy."

Claire said the kids have something they need to tell you.

I thought to myself, "This ought to be good."

Lainey spoke up, and said "Mom, Drew and I had unprotected sex last night, I know it was stupid, and I won't do it again, I promise, but I need the morning after pill. I am running out of time."

All of the color drained out of my face. I felt like I was going to faint.

I didn't speak for several minutes because this was a discussion I didn't want to have.

Lainey started to cry and said she knew I was disappointed in her.

Contrary to what everyone thought, I wasn't mad.

The three of them were staring at me.

I began by saying, "I'm not disappointed in you, Lainey, and I will take you to the drugstore to get the morning after pill, but I feel like I need to share something with you. Drew and Claire, can you give us a moment? I need to talk with my daughter privately."

Claire and Drew complied, and my daughter and I sat down across from each other. I let her know that I should have shared this with her before but that it would explain a lot.

"I met your dad when I was a little younger than you are. We were high-school sweethearts, prom king and queen, and voted most likely to succeed."

Lainey interrupted me. "I know mom, you have told me this story a million times."

"Let me continue. I had always dreamed about becoming a veterinarian. I had been accepted to the University of Pennsylvania and Dad, who wanted to study dentistry, was accepted to Drexel University. We were only 27 minutes apart and always planned on staying together. The future was full of possibilities until

I got pregnant with you in my sophomore year. There was never a question as to whether I would have you, but I had to decide if I was going to finish school and, at the end of the day, I couldn't do both. Veterinary school was harder than I anticipated, and there was so much practical work that I just didn't see how I could do both, so I dropped out. Dad didn't ask me to. We discussed it, but I thought it would be the best thing in the long run if we were going to stay together.

Don't misunderstand me, I love our family.

I know you think I am tough on you. I'm not complaining about my life, I feel blessed, but my dream of becoming a veterinarian got crushed in one night. Your brother Matthew came along four years later and that was that.

Dad is a very successful dentist and we do very well, but I have made it my mission to make sure that you don't miss out on anything. I think I would have loved a career. That time was very difficult, Lainey, and I started drinking, which is not dissimilar to throwing up. It is a way to ease the pain.

I know you judge me and think I am a hard-ass, but I have my reasons. So, maybe this will help you understand why I ride you so hard."

Lainey was clearly shocked. "So you resent me and make my life hell!"

"No, I don't resent you, I love you, but I don't want you to miss out on your dreams because you made a poor judgement call. I guess my methods of conveying this didn't work since you did the same thing I did at an earlier age.

Let's go to the drugstore, but I do hope you kids have learned your lesson."

We got ready to leave and I walked up to Claire.

"Please spare me your parenting advice. I know you think you know everything, but I know how to parent my daughter. I do appreciate that you encouraged them to be truthful and not let them do anything behind my back, but we aren't friends."

It actually felt really good to get that out. I was ashamed to admit my history to Lainey, but perhaps it would allow us to start over.

When we got in the car Lainey asked me why I had never told her any of this.

I told her that I wasn't proud that I had to drop out of college, and I didn't want her to question if she was wanted. She most definitely was. I always wanted children, she was part of the plan, just not so early, I said.

Lainey got the pill, and I made her an appointment with my gynecologist.

Gary

I got a call from Drew, and he was upset. He told me that he and Lainey had had sex.

I wanted to give him a high-five. Was it wrong that I felt proud? That feeling was short-lived since he then proceeded to tell me they didn't use protection.

"What the hell were you thinking, Drew? We have discussed this a million times.

Clearly, you weren't thinking so let's get mom and figure out what we are going to do.

How is Lainey handling this?"

He then told me that Claire already called Lainey's mom and they got her the morning after pill.

While of course I was relieved, I wondered why I was just hearing about this now. Haven't I been dating my wife, living in a crappy apartment, talking about my feelings to make sure we were communicating?

She hated Ginger, but she told Ginger before me. What was I missing?

I got Claire on the line and blurted out, "I thought we were making progress, yet why am I hearing about Drew and Lainey after the situation has already been resolved? Why does Ginger get a call before I do?"

I couldn't help but tell her that I was frustrated that she didn't call me first. She apologized and said that they had to act quickly because the morning after pill must be taken within 24 hours.

"I get that, Claire, but it would have taken you five minutes to call me before you called Ginger.

I mean you don't even like Ginger but thought of her first."

"I thought of her first since it involved her daughter, and I didn't want our son to end up getting his girlfriend pregnant. I'm sorry you are so offended."

"You're missing the point, Claire. If you haven't noticed, we are separated because of not involving each other in big decisions. I thought we were making great strides, but this just feels like we are reverting back to old bad habits."

"I'm sorry that you feel that way, it wasn't what I intended, but this was a unique situation. I panicked and I had a lapse in judgement."

I heard the words, but they sounded a little empty like she was appeasing me rather than acknowledging that we may have more work to do than she had anticipated.

I decided to reach out to Ginger myself. I wanted to talk about Drew and Lainey but not with Claire. I was too pissed off.

I found Ginger's number in the White Pages and gave her a call.

Ginger picked up on the second ring. I told her who I was and her first words were, "Jesus, can't you Holdens leave me alone? Now what?"

I was startled by her tone but I told her I was upset about the kids and wanted to see if she wanted to talk.

She said she wasn't happy either, but what's done is done. Lainey took the morning after pill and she would be fine.

I said I wasn't terribly surprised that they had had sex but I was furious that they didn't use protection.

"They could have ruined their lives with that type of careless behavior."

"Don't I know it."

"Are you going to punish Lainey?"

"I don't think that will be necessary. I pretty much told her that she was an accident and I had to drop out of school when I got pregnant with her."

"Wow, that is harsh."

"Sometimes reality is."

"Don't get me wrong. I have a nice life, but it hasn't been easy, and I do feel like I missed out on something, which I conveyed to Lainey."

"How did Lainey take it?"

"She is angry at me, but what else is new?"

Ginger asked me if Claire had told me about Lainey's bulimia. I let her know I had heard and that she had started going to Reclaim You for the teen program.

"Imagine me having to hear that from Claire," Ginger said.

"Apparently, Lainey confided in Drew that she has an eating disorder and she is blaming it on me. Oh, and Lainey feels better talking to your pill-popping wife since I am the one causing it."

"Ginger, you are talking about my wife and although I'm not too pleased with her right now either, I find your words offensive."

"You know what is offensive? Having my daughter talk to your wife when I have sacrificed everything for that girl. Your wife who tried to get me to buy Adderall at a PTA meeting."

"I'm sorry that you and Claire are dealing with this, but we all have our demons. I already struggled with addiction, and I resent the fact that my daughter went to your wife instead of me. She isn't the only one who has experience with addiction. I have been in AA for 15 years."

"I'm sorry, I didn't know anything about the drugs until it was too late."

"Well, that's usually the way"

"Why do you hate Claire so much? I mean she was trying to do the right thing by telling you in both instances, the eating disorder and the sex. I get that you didn't want to buy Adderall, but is she really that loathsome?"

"Again, not your business, but I have had my own struggles with addiction, and the fact that I can't go to a PTA meeting without a temptation is inexcusable."

"I had no idea."

"Well you shouldn't have any idea, this is my business, and I do my best to stay away from situations that could trigger me. The PTA is supposed to be a safe space.

Although I think Drew is a great kid, this is more involvement with your family than I need."

"If you don't mind me asking, how did you and your husband get through the addiction? While I think Claire and I are making strides, I have a lot of anger that I am having trouble dealing with," I said.

"Look, no one is perfect, but my husband Pete went to Al-Anon to talk to other people who had a similar situation. My issues with alcohol definitely put a strain on our marriage, but again, this was many years ago."

"Does he still go to meetings?"

"He doesn't anymore. I have been sober for 15 years, but you should get some support for yourself. The alcohol was a vice for me, not the actual problem. It became a problem, but it was more like a symptom that I was feeling out of control.

Claire is in the throes of recovery which is an up-and-down battle. Although you two need to communicate, you need someone objective to talk to as well."

"I see how that could help. I like talking to you Ginger, you don't sugarcoat anything and I appreciate you listening."

She then told me that she hoped Claire and I could work through our issues, reminding me that she was living proof it could be done.

Claire

Gary called and I could immediately sense something was wrong.

He was furious. He told me that Drew had called him but wanted to know why I didn't think to call as soon as I had found out about the kids. I said it had just happened and I was literally picking up the phone to tell him and he beat me to it.

He replied that it didn't just happen and that I already had worked with Ginger on a resolution and didn't even tell him until it was resolved.

He then told me he called Ginger to discuss the consequences.

"Gary, you know I hate Ginger, " I said, "why are you calling her to discuss our son instead of me?"

"I could be asking you the same thing."

"What the hell does that mean?"

"Nothing, I am just disappointed that we are here again."

"Ginger said it is going to take you a while to recover from your substance abuse issues, and that I need to be patient with you."

"Why are you talking to Ginger about me? I barely understand why you reached out to her to begin with, but now you are talking to her about us?"

"Oh, relax Claire, she had an issue with alcohol a while back too so she was just giving me a little advice as to what I can expect."

I was stunned. I had been planning on inviting Gary over to look at baby pictures, as this whole situation made me realize that Drew is more of a man than a boy, but F him.

I thought I needed a meeting. I checked out the Reclaim You schedule and headed over there to find one that I could pop into.

After the meeting let out, I tried to see if I could get in with my therapist. She seemed to be booked solid. This was the worst I have felt in months.

I thought we were really making progress, but it seemed like Gary still had a lot of anger bottled up.

I would have felt better if he had spoken to just about anyone else other than Ginger.

She was pretty clear that she didn't want much to do with my family. I bet she was doing this just to get under my skin.

Ginger

I was shocked to get a call from Gary Holden, but it was actually nice to talk to someone about the kids. It really hurt me that Lainey thought I was so hard to talk to. I had given up so much to make sure she had every opportunity available to her and she looked at me as the enemy.

It was sort of odd that I confided in Gary about my own battles with addiction. I rarely talked about that anymore, as it seemed like a lifetime ago. Thankfully, it was a closed chapter. I mean, once an addict, always an addict, but I haven't had a slip-up in 15 years. My issues started when I was alone with Lainey while Pete was bartending after school so we could pay the rent. I was lonely and I turned to alcohol sometimes to help me get through. I didn't get into the details with Gary, just enough to let him know that you don't go to rehab for six weeks and end up better.

Every day is a new day to conquer. When a curve ball gets thrown into your everyday routine, sometimes you just want to reach for that drink or, in Claire's case, that pill.

I just advised him to talk to someone or maybe go to an Al-Anon meeting.

I let him know I didn't hate Claire but she just brought up some bad memories for me from a time in my life that was filled with depression and a lack of control.

I told him that I didn't feel I owed her an explanation and I just wanted to keep away from her. But of course our kids are dating. Murphy's law.

When Lainey got home, I sat her down and apologized for being tough on her but I was trying to shield her from mistakes I have made.

"I wonder if you think it is a good idea to get so serious with Drew at such a young age," I told her. "Don't get me wrong, Lainey, he is a lovely boy, and I don't hold it against him that you decided to have sex. I am just saying you are planning to go away to school, and this has clearly gotten very intense. You have a whole lifetime ahead of you, why don't you guys take some time to reflect on what just happened?"

She told me she loved Drew and knew that they had made a mistake but didn't want to break up. I decided not to push it since Lainey seemed to do the opposite of what I suggested, so I let her know that if she wanted to talk, I was there.

I suspect she still won't talk to me, but at least I got my perspective out there.

Claire

I was still having a hard time trying to understand why Gary would reach out to Ginger. It made no sense. They weren't friends prior to our kids dating, and he knows that I have struggled with Ginger even prior to this incident.

I was sort of surprised to learn that she has had her own substance abuse issues, considering she seems very judgmental of me, but again, not my biggest gripe.

I am still filled with so many insecurities I don't need her talking with my husband about anything. I was feeling like things were really heading in a good direction, now I was anxious since this happened with the kids.

I was considering having Gary over and working on a game plan, but he was so quick to assume that I wasn't going to include him that I decided to forgo the invitation and just look through my old photos alone, perhaps with a glass of wine?

Although my issue wasn't with alcohol, I knew that drinking probably wasn't the wisest choice, but I needed something to soothe my nerves.

I poured myself a glass and pulled out my albums from when Drew was just a baby. Time was going by so quickly.

There were a ton of family shots, and I started to cry. Why was this so hard?

The wine was relaxing me, and I poured myself one more glass. I was starting to feel more settled, and I decided to call Gary.

He picked up and I told him I was sorry. I didn't mean to make a decision without him, but I was just trying to fix things.

He told me I wasn't responsible for fixing everything. Especially on my own. If the two of us were going to make it, I had to include him in everything. Just as he owed me the same courtesy.

I was very weepy; I blamed the alcohol.

I asked him if he wanted to come over. He hesitated and asked me if I had been drinking. I told him I was having a glass of wine.

He then questioned whether that was a good idea, so I told him not to bother coming over.

I was a grown-ass adult, and I could do whatever I wanted.

I hung up and cried myself to sleep.

Gary

Well, this wasn't going the way that I had anticipated. Claire and I had had a lot of nice get-togethers recently, and now I felt like I was back at square one.

I took what Ginger had said to heart. Six weeks of rehab couldn't possibly fix everything, which I knew, but the fact that Claire didn't think to call me made me wonder if we were making progress. As Ginger said, this wasn't something we saw coming, and when Claire felt out of control she panicked, which might be why she didn't think to call me. She just wanted to fix it.

I decided to find an Al-Anon meeting.

Turns out there were meetings all over the place. I chose to drive to one a little farther away from me because I didn't want to run into anyone I knew.

I chose a beginner's meeting. There were eight other people and thankfully no one I recognized. The meeting opened with the Serenity Prayer and the suggested Al-Anon welcome.

We were assured that everything discussed was confidential and that anonymity was an important principle of the program.

It was emphasized while this was spiritual it wasn't a religious meeting, so we wouldn't be discussing religious beliefs.

Next, we discussed that this was an open forum and everyone would have an opportunity to talk. We went around the room and talked about what had brought us there, and I talked about what was going on with Claire and how we seemed to be on a good trajectory and then life threw us a curve ball and we were right back to where we started. Or at least that was how it felt to me.

Although she hadn't taken Adderall, she was drinking when she called me to continue the discussion around what we were at odds over. Although I had served her wine at the dinner at my apartment, I was starting to think she shouldn't be drinking. The feedback from the room was that Claire was most likely still struggling and that I had every right to my feelings, but the only way to move forward was through discussion, not fighting.

I knew this was true, but when I started discussing what had happened, I got mad all over again and ended up yelling. I had thought we were making progress, but I wanted her to reach out to me when something was wrong. It wasn't clear why she still wasn't. We had been talking about how that was how we were going to repair our marriage. She agreed and then Drew has a problem, and she called Ginger?

As we went around the room, I heard what other people were dealing with and I knew I wasn't alone, and that others had it worse. But I was still a little down.

I decided that I was going to call her in the morning to see if we could discuss what had happened and I was going to ask her to refrain from drinking in addition to the pills.

She had only been sober for a short time and I would feel better knowing she was clear-headed while we were working though our issues.

Surprisingly, I did have a solid night's sleep and I called Claire. She picked up and I started by apologizing for snapping at her.

She told me she was sorry as well. She should have called me first, she said, but was so worried about getting Lainey the morning after pill that she had been hasty. She promised me that it wasn't that she didn't think of me.

I felt better and then said I didn't have the right to ask but I would really prefer if she refrained from drinking. I thought alcohol could prove a slippery slope, and in solidarity I wouldn't drink in her presence.

She didn't say anything for quite some time.

When she spoke again, she asked if that was really necessary? I told her yes but that she should think about asking what her therapist thought.

She agreed to do that.

She then asked if I wanted to come over to the house and look at some of Drew's baby pictures. I told her I would love that.

I felt infinitely better, and I was going to tell her that I went to an Al-Anon meeting as well.

Lainey

My mom just blew my mind. I had no idea that she had career goals aside from being a Mrs.

I actually felt kind of sad when she shared her story with me. I never really sat and did the math, but she definitely was on the younger side of the moms.

She was so well-coifed and put together, I just thought she put in more effort. But she could be a good five to 10 years younger than my friends' mothers.

Regardless, the point was that I saw that by being careless I could have really screwed things up. I thought

Drew was equally freaked out when we considered that I could have gotten pregnant. I did love him, but he told me that he really wanted to go to SUNY Stony Brook to study pre-med, and I had my dreams of going to the University of Michigan.

After the recent scare things felt different between us. I couldn't put my finger on it, but if I had learned one thing from the conversation with my mother, I had to follow my dreams.

Drew and I needed to discuss our future, and maybe it was time to take a break. As sad as that made me feel, I was excited to start the next chapter of my life.

I also needed to apologize to Drew's mom. I had been a bit standoffish to her lately. I was mad that she had told my mother, but I knew I had put her in a tough position.

She had introduced me to a group at Reclaim You that was really helping me manage my bulimia. There were a lot of kids in this group. We were all puking for different reasons. Some did it for weight, but whatever the end goal it all revolved around control. My mother could only control so much, but if I wanted, I could make myself throw up and she couldn't stop me. It was weird, but it sort of made sense.

I hadn't binged in close to six weeks.

I guessed Drew and I would see how we felt when we get back from our first break if we tried the long-distance thing. I would never regret my time with him, no matter how it turned out.

Drew

I loved Lainey, but I had been thinking about us being at different schools, and it was hard to imagine us staying together.

I was getting the impression that she was thinking the same thing. I loved her, there was no question, but I felt so much pressure from every aspect of my life.

I felt terrible that my dad didn't know what was going on, I had just assumed my mom had told him since that was always how it used to be. They were both mad at each other.

I thought I might dorm at Stony Brook. It wouldn't suck to have a fresh start and get away from everyone. I knew my dad's first screening since the diagnosis was coming up and I was sure that was weighing on his mind.

I couldn't help but think that I could have easily been having a screening every three months too.

I felt guilty and relieved.

He must be freaking out, so perhaps my mom was trying to save him from another worry, but the house was just so tense.

My mom kept trying to hug me, which was so annoying. Ever since Lainey and I had told her we had sex, she kept telling me how cute I was as a baby and was making me look at pictures.

Parents are freakin' weird.

Lainey and I were meeting up after school, which was the first time I was seeing her since the scare. My gut was telling me this is a goodbye, and I was actually OK with it. I did love her, but we were young and if we were meant to be together, we would be.

We did help each other through some tough times, and I would never forget that. But I was excited to start over.

Claire

Once again, my stomach was in knots to see my husband, whom I have been with for more than half of my life. The whole Drew situation made me realize that I still have a ways to go. Don't get me wrong, I have made tremendous strides, but I wasn't prepared for that curve ball and in some part of me I wanted to escape. The interesting thing is I wasn't craving a pill but a drink. Gary was all over me and saw that I was heading down a bad path. I have to give him credit. He knows me, perhaps better than I know myself.

Gary arrived, and he is still just so handsome. I invited him in and offered him a soda. I wished it were a wine, but I was behaving.

We sat down and I apologized again.

I explained that I didn't really have a good excuse for not calling him first.

I acknowledged he was right, that it used to be automatic.

I guess I got out of the habit, and I promised to try and start doing that again. He appreciated it and asked me if I would come with him to his screening.

I assured him that I would be right by his side. I asked him if he worried about getting cancer all of the time since being told he had the gene.

He told me that it was always in the back of his mind. I hugged him and said that it must be really stressful and I was sorry we hadn't really discussed it.

He asked me about my recovery, and I told him honestly, I thought it was going better than it was, and the thing with Drew made me feel like I was right back to where I started.

He said that it made total sense but if the two of us were really going to mend I had to lean on him rather than pills or alcohol. And he said he should have told me how nervous he was about the screening.

Drew was going to be leaving the nest, he said, and we would have to turn to each other.

After a few minutes of just comforting each other, I asked him if he would like to look through the pictures I pulled out from when Drew was little.

We started looking and realized what an amazing lifetime of memories we had created.

I turned to him and said we were so blessed, so how did we get so far apart?

He said it was going to be OK and that we were finding our way back to each other. I nodded, but still just didn't understand what had happened.

Then it dawned on me of how scared I was of growing old. I could see all of these amazing things coming to a close, the prospect of Gary getting a bad diagnosis, and I was afraid of the next chapter.

I decided to tell Gary about my fears.

He told me he felt the same way, but if we conquered this together and really kept sharing our feelings, it wouldn't be so bad.

I said it was all going so fast.

He agreed but wanted us to stay present instead of anticipating what could be, otherwise we would end up wasting precious time.

All of a sudden, I just wanted to be as close to him as possible, so I kissed him. I had no intention of being intimate with Gary, but I decided to follow my heart.

I wasn't thinking about whether or not I would have an orgasm, I wasn't worried about if it would screw up my recovery, I was just living in the moment—and it was beautiful. I asked him to stay, and he said he would love to.

We both slept really well and when the morning arrived, I had no regrets and from the looks of it he didn't either.

Gary

I decided to give Henri a call since I was days away from my first screening. It felt selfish to call him, but he was the only one who could truly understand what I was feeling.

I asked him how he was doing.

"Gary, I am having a very hard time with the loss of Jean and anticipating my results. I feel really low."

"Henri, you have every reason to be anxious, but statistics say the older you are without having the cancer, the better your odds of not getting it.

"Men are also 20 percent less likely to inherit as well. That is what I keep telling myself as I prepare for the screening."

"It is an unfortunate hand we've been dealt," he said, adding that he had been in touch with Bill and Loretta and they were missing Jean terribly too.

I needed to reach out to them but I was going to wait until the screening was behind me. Then it occurred to me that the waiting was going to be awful, so maybe I should take Claire to meet them while we waited for the results.

I ran the idea past Henri, who said he thought it was a marvelous idea. I asked him if he would consider coming too.

As much as he would like to have given us all a hug, until his English got better, we wouldn't be able to really communicate.

I told him to hang in there and I would let him know if we were going to take the trip. I got Bill on the phone, and he did sound down. I asked him if he would like a visit, and he said it would be wonderful. I told him I was going to bring Claire if she agreed.

The next morning, I floated the idea by Claire, and she was ecstatic to take the trip. She agreed that we needed a change of scenery and seemed really excited to meet my family. I then called Bill and figured out the dates and got ready for our road trip.

Claire

We started to plan our trip and I was really looking forward to meeting Gary's half-sister and brother-in-law.

I wished I had had the opportunity to meet Jean, but I could tell how impactful the time Gary spent with Jean was. I thought the only reason he has given me a second chance was because of the conversations he had with her. She encouraged Gary not to try to fight the battle on his own, and I would forever be indebted.

After a scenic ride, we were greeted with a warm reception from Bill and Loretta. The drive was long, but we were too excited to rest.

We washed up and proceeded to sit around the table and get to know each other.

I could see where Gary got his charm. There was something about this family that was so warm.

We asked them how they had been coping with Jean's loss, and it was evident that they were both struggling.

We invited them to share some memories. Gary already knew a lot, but I wanted to learn more. I asked Bill how they met.

Here's what he told us.

It was the summer of 1973. Jean was giving a birthday party for her good friend Cathy. My sister, Cindy, was invited and asked if it was OK if she brought her brother. I was so glad that Jean said yes. The more the merrier. I was taken with Jean. She was the prettiest girl I had ever met. It may sound corny, but it was like the old saying, Love at first sight. Young love, everybody said, it will never last, after all I was 17 and Jean was 15. That night was the beginning of the best 48 years of my life. Jean can tell you the same thing.

Bill shared a video that Jean had made for him four days before her death. Their love was inspiring.

They say their voice is the first thing that you forget. I watch her video at least once a week because I never want to forget her voice.

We were married two years later on June 28, 1975. I was 19 and Jean was 17. We wanted to get married while we were young so when our kids were grown we would still be young enough to enjoy each other's company and be able to do things together. Our oldest son, Rob, was born on April 30, 1977, and our youngest, Joe, was born on November 10, 1979.

Rob and his wife Karen have blessed us with three grandchildren. Tanner is 18, Helaina is 8 and Declan is 5. Jean thrived on being a Granny. They were her pride and joy.

Even though 'J'—that is what I called her all through our marriage—was only 5' 1", you did not want to make her mad or you would hear about it. LOL. Don't get me wrong, she could laugh at herself about her small size. She called herself 'vertically challenged.' J was small but she was mighty.

I remember when Jean and I first started dating. We went camping at Green Lake with my family. While there, one of my brothers and I grabbed Jean by the arms and legs and threw her in the water off the wharf. I didn't know it at the time, but Jean was deathly afraid of the water. Apparently, she had a bad experience when she was younger. We had to jump in and help her out. She never spoke to me the rest of the weekend. Lucky for me, she eventually forgave me, after much groveling.

Even though Jean, as well as all health-care workers, are advised not to become emotionally attached to their clients, I witnessed and can recall numerous times J would come home and shed tears as she told me about her clients' struggles and their fights to get better. Jean was a very emotionally caring person. She always put others' needs ahead of her own, be it family or friends.

J loved games. We would spend hours playing Scrabble, kings in the corner, poker or cribbage, although I never won a cribbage game against her. We were diehard Ottawa Senators fans. We had game date nights where we would have dinner at Bert's and then go to the game. We also looked forward to our monthly dinner and a movie date nights. I believe I sent you a picture of Jean *in a booth at Moxie's. That is the last date night we had before she became too ill.*

Although I only witnessed this occasionally, apparently J had a pretty warped sense of humor. Her close friends or maybe even Loretta could attest to this more than me. They used to get together whenever possible for a girls only day.

J was an avid reader, who could spend hours just relaxing with a cup of tea and a good book. Something I picked up from her over the years."

I thought back on the many nights that Gary and I had gone to dinner and the movies or broke out the Scrabble or Rummy cube. I didn't know this woman, but I felt such a loss after listening to Bill recount their life.

Bill told us that her oncologist had said in his 21-year career, Jean was only the second case of Li-Fraumeni Syndrome that he had treated.

I had such a sense of who Jean was from Bill's recollections. I hoped it was OK to ask, but I wondered how they had found out about the syndrome. I asked if he would share the journey.

He nodded.

After a routine mammogram they discovered a lump on Jean's right breast, and they performed a biopsy. This led to a number of tests where it was discovered that Jean carried the genetic disorder Li-Fraumeni Syndrome. After meeting with an oncologist who told us that if we had waited Jean would have been gone within a year, it was decided to have surgery. Jean had the surgery, which involved removing the tumors as well as the lymph nodes and her nipple. Her road to recovery was long and hard with all of the chemotherapy.

Three years later it was discovered that J also suffered from Leiomyosarcoma. Apparently, this is a soft tissue sarcoma and can spread to different organs. Jean's cancer had returned and spread to her spleen. At this time, she was given one to three years. She saw another oncologist at this time and was told one to three years was very optimistic. It was probably like six months to a year. After the surgery to remove Jean's spleen and a portion of her pancreas, the long process of chemo treatments started all over again.

These took quite a toll on her as she was tired and very sick. With the treatments, Jean started to feel somewhat better. However, just seven months later they discovered that the cancer had now spread to her liver where they found six tumors. They called it metastatic cancer and that it was inoperable. Jean decided that she wanted as much time as she could get and, being the fighter that she was, opted to take chemo treatments again. So, she started months of treatments and tests. After three months of treatments, they performed another CAT scan where they found the tumors on her liver had grown. A different treatment was tried but still the tumors grew. In April of this past year, we spoke to the oncologist. Jean asked if there was anything else we could try and we were told there was one more option, but the side effects would be worse than the disease, and the chances of it working were less than 2 percent. We talked *it over for quite a while and decided that there were things we wanted to do before it was too late, so Jean opted out of the final treatment. The oncologist agreed with us that we should take the holiday we wanted to.*

We had always wanted to do the Lake Superior circle tour, so we did in June of last year. Unfortunately, due to COVID, we were only able to do the Canadian side of Lake Superior. We had booked a dinner boat cruise in Parry Sound while on the trip, but it was canceled due to Covid. That was very disappointing. After that, we went to Prince Edward Island to visit Jean's half sister and her husband for a week. Again, we had a fantastic time. One of Jean's favorite things to do there was searching for the shorelines looking for sea glass.

Bill's eyes were misty, and I felt like I knew Jean.

In September when things were opening up again and COVID restrictions were easing up, we discovered that the boat cruises were back up and running in Parry Sound. I mentioned them to Jean, and she said, 'Let's do it.' I was unsure if it was a good idea with Jean's health deteriorating. She looked at me and said, 'This may be the last little trip we take together so I want to do it.' So, we did.

We had one more dinner and a movie date night before Jean's health got too bad.

Her health started to go downhill quicker after that. My son and I decorated the outside of the house with a crazy amount of lights last year at Christmas for her to see as we knew that it would be her last.

I knew that Jean wanted to stay home as long as possible, and I did my best to see to that. I had taken compassionate leave from work to be with her and look after her. We spoke about that there would come a time when I would just not be able to do it anymore and agreed that when the time came, she would go to the hospital.

I like to think that I did my best in that respect with feeding her, bathing her, dressing her and trying to keep her comfortable.

Unfortunately, the time came, and our family physician paid us a visit and it was decided that Jean would enter palliative care at the Carleton Place Memorial Hospital. My son and I drove Jean to the hospital, and she was taken off all of her meds save for the morphine for her pain. The first week in the hospital she had all of the nurses singing and dancing when they came into her room as she liked to listen to her music a little loud.

Bill laughed at the memory.

Then the inevitable happened and she started to get weaker quickly. She was able to make me a video that I will share. It was a 'goodbye video' that I can't seem to get through without crying, although I have watched it hundreds of times.

Two days after she created that video, she was pretty much unresponsive. The last thing she said to me was, 'And you are my man.' While brushing my cheek with her hand after I fed her some applesauce and told her she was my gal, always was and always will be my gal.

At this point Gary, Loretta and I were sobbing.

The day she passed the entire family was with her throughout the day, including you, Gary, and Henri over FaceTime to say their goodbyes. I pray she heard them. I had been staying at the hospital every night for the past few nights. Loretta and her daughter were the last to leave and then Jean took her last breath. I held her hand and told her how much I loved her. I will love her until I take my last breath. I thank God for letting Jean be part of my life for the last 48 years. I miss her terribly.

It was hard to regain our composure after Bill shared the details of their journey, but I understood that lifetime love and I wasn't going to let ours slip away.

Loretta sat nodding her head and smiling when thinking about her beloved sister.

Loretta echoed Bill's sentiments. She had already shared a lot with Gary on their first visit, but she reiterated that she was the tomboy of the pair and Jean was more studious. She often got Jean into situations that she couldn't get out of. Like getting stuck in trees, visiting haunted houses, and other mischievous adventures kids got into.

They used to finish each other's sentences, and the void would never be filled. However, their memories would live on forever.

After a lovely meal we decide to get some rest, and planned to do some sightseeing in the morning.

Gary and I shared a bed for the first time in over a year.

We were both exhausted, and fell asleep rather quickly, but in each other's arms.

The arms I had taken for granted.

I would never do that again.

We woke up well rested and looked forward to seeing the places that Jean, Loretta and their families had spent most of their time. It was a tight-knit community where people seemed to know each other.

The rest of the visit was spent reminiscing and learning more about Gary's roots.

When it was finally time to leave, we thanked them for their hospitality and promised to stay in touch.

On the drive back we talked about Bill and Loretta, and the similarities that could only be genetic, and then we addressed the elephant in the room. We were going home to the test results.

There was no way to predict what we would hear, but we decided that we would deal with whatever the news was together.

PART 3

Gary

The trip to Canada was amazing, and Claire and I were doing really well. She now came with me to every screening, which had become sort of routine but were still very nerve-wracking.

I had to get:

- *Annual whole-body MRIs*
- *Annual brain MRIs*
- *Brain MRI with contrast*
- *Brain MRI without contrast*
- *Abdominal and pelvic ultrasound every three to four months*
- *Physical exam every six months*
- *Annual dermatology exam*
- *Colonoscopy every two to five years*
- *Endoscopy and esophagus and stomach every two to five years*

As we drove to my ultrasound, I told her I was grateful that Drew didn't have to go through all of this shit. There were so many tests that I felt like I could never relax. There was a constant worry in the back of my mind.

Claire said she worried about me constantly too.

It had been almost a year that I have been going through these screenings. Things were feeling almost back to "normal."

We now had dinner together every night. I have decided that I would cook some nights too. Although when it was my turn to cook my meals were simple, I was sticking to my promise of sharing in the work.

Sometimes we even cooked together.

We started taking cooking classes on the weekends as we continued to date. It was fun, and we were both enjoying the fruits of our therapy and efforts.

Claire had been doing amazing with her recovery. She attended meetings three nights a week and seemed genuinely happy again.

We were communicating better than ever and made a concerted effort to check in with each other and pointedly ask each other what we were dealing with.

I struggled a lot with the knowledge of Li-Fraumeni Syndrome, and she was empathetic. We reminded each other that we had to live in the present and not waste time anticipating.

Finally, I was invited to move back home where I belong. I will never take being by Claire's side for granted again.

Although our days became almost routine, I went to bed thanking God for every moment we had together. I thanked him for the gift of finding my family, for Drew, and for giving me a second chance with my wonderful family.

We FaceTimed with Bill and Loretta weekly. With every call they seemed to be healing. Of course, we still talked about Jean on every call, but instead of tears there was now laughter recalling her sense of humor. Henri finally got his test results back and was elated to learn he didn't have the gene. I sensed he was hesitant to tell me, but I was thrilled to learn he didn't have to live with the knowledge that he had this looming disease in his body.

I didn't want to tell Claire, but I was noticing a little pain in my abdominal area and after all of our therapy, I had to share.

She insisted I tell the doctor.

When I got to the screening, I mentioned the pain to my doctor and Claire was by my side. He proceeded to press around the abdominal area, and I could see by the look on his face that he had felt something.

He looked up and said there was definitely something present in the right lower section of my abdomen.

But we needed to move forward with the screening.

I went through the tests and as usual had to hurry up and wait for the results. The doctor said he would be in touch in the next couple of days.

Since Drew was living at Stony Brook University, we decided to meet for dinner and to see how he was doing. We met up at a local restaurant. Although close to our house, Drew had decided to dorm on campus, which was a great idea. He had the security of knowing he could come home at any time, but he was learning how to live independently.

We all hugged and sat down at the table, and I immediately asked how school was going. His face lit up, and he said he was loving everything about his classes and his social life.

Claire asked him if he had been in touch with Lainey. He said they had spoken a couple of times, and it had been friendly. But they were both enjoying college life and agreed that their breakup was the right thing to do.

I was so proud of my boy. I should say my "young man," but he will always be my little boy. He asked me about my screening and I refrained from telling him about the pain in my abdomen until I knew something.

He has had a lot of scares in his young life, and I vowed not to keep facts from him or Claire again, but right now I didn't know what this was—and it could be a hernia for all I knew.

The meal was wonderful, the mood was good, and we left our boy to go back to the family home.

We poured a glass of sparkling cider, talked about Drew a little more, and Claire said she was so happy I was back home.

I looked into her eyes, kissed her deeply and said nothing made me happier than being with her. I couldn't believe how far we had come, and I was so grateful that we had done the work.

We headed to bed, and in the morning raced around like usual, grabbed our travel mugs and headed off to our jobs.

Claire had decided not to become a social worker and continued on in her advertising career successfully. After discussing how wonderful the therapy was, we both decided that she could appreciate it without having to become a therapist. In fact, refraining from jumping into another thing was actually a sign that she was getting better.

I think she will be a lifetime member at Reclaim You, which was a wonderful resource in addition to our partnership. You couldn't have too many outlets. Recognizing that she could be a patient, and not have to work, there was definite progress.

Two days later the doctor called and suggested I head back into the office for another visit. This freaked me out, and I asked him what was going on. He said that we would discuss it at our visit.

I told Claire and of course she accompanied me. We sat down and the doctor told us that the ultrasound concluded that I had a serious liver condition. There were two masses and cirrhosis was presentable.

I barely drank—could this be another thing that my stupid father passed down?

I asked the doctor and he thought it was unlikely that it was hereditary but set me up with a liver specialist to examine further.

That was it? I got one moment of happiness and then another crisis. Claire squeezed my hand and said we shouldn't anticipate the worst. We should wait to see what the specialist said.

I met with the specialist within a week, and she was perplexed with the liver damage as well. She asked me multiple times if I abused alcohol, and my story was consistent. I did not.

We scheduled a CT scan and after further examination the good news was I didn't have liver disease, but I wasn't out of the woods. It looked like I had cancer.

Next, I had to have a biopsy. I met with the hospital's oncologist. He confirmed that my biopsy came back malignant. Of course, with Li-Fraumeni Syndrome no one was that surprised, except for me.

It turned out it was a sarcoma, and Stony Brook wasn't equipped to treat this so I would have to figure out how I was going to start the battle for my life.

This was more than my brain could handle. Claire and I went home, and we cried together. She assured me that we would battle this as a united front, and I wouldn't be alone.

I thought back to the little I witnessed Jean go through and I was scared. Why me? We knew we would have to tell Drew.

We didn't want to do it over the phone, so we called and invited him home for Sunday dinner. He was so thrilled that I had moved back in, and of course he had a ton of laundry that he could do while we visited.

We sit down at the table after the first load was in the washing machine, and told Drew we had to tell him something.

His face grew serious. I let him know that it seemed like something had shown up on the scan and it was cancer.

I proceeded to tell him all of the things we knew thus far, which wasn't that much, and let him know that I would have to start going into New York City for treatment.

He made it his mission to learn as much as he possibly could about sarcomas, and I promised to keep him in the loop as I learned more about my fate.

I was still feeling OK, but that was because I hadn't begun any treatment yet. That would follow shortly.

As a family, after investigating we decided I would do my treatment at Memorial Sloan Kettering Cancer Center.

They let me know that my cancer was called retroperitoneal, meaning it was located in the abdominal region, up against the back abdominal wall.

Although big, it was determined that my treatment would require radiation only, which was a relief. I was concerned because early on I had been told I needed to avoid radiation.

I signed up for 25 daily sessions. Claire and I both took leaves from our jobs. Me on disability and her on the Family Leave Act.

I convinced Drew to stay in school even though he wanted to be with me. I assured him that the best help he could offer was to get that degree as a doctor and find a cure.

After reviewing the scan, the doctor told me that the tumor was the size of a softball.

That was big. I knew a lot about baseball, and this was even bigger.

I decided I had to tell Bill, Loretta and Henri. I knew they would be worried, but I thought they deserved to know.

They all offered to visit, but the radiation and pending surgery were already overwhelming, and Claire and I decided that provided everything went OK, it would be better for them to come when I was on the mend.

They understood but made it very clear that they were willing and able to make the trip if Claire needed support.

That was the beauty of family. I had just met them, but it was as if they had always been a part of my life.

The daily radiation trips were hard and took a lot out of me. Claire made the trip to and from with me without complaint.

Although feeling tired, I was OK until one night while Claire and I were eating some soup and I got really dizzy. I barely made it to the bathroom in time to empty my stomach. I panicked and started to hyperventilate. Claire called 911 and within 30 minutes I was in the ER getting another CT scan.

The scan showed I had a pulmonary embolism. Of course I did.

I stayed in the hospital for three days and was shown how to inject a needle into my abdomen to release a blood thinner to dissipate the embolism.

I had to stop the radiation while dealing with this. My tumor hadn't shrunk but had actually grown.

I resumed the radiation and finally was ready for surgery to get the tumor out. It was finally small enough to proceed.

I got to pre-op two days before to learn about what the 15-hour surgery would entail. I was so worried, not just about myself but about Drew and Claire as well.

They both planned on being at the hospital the entire time, and I didn't protest because I know if, God forbid, it was one of them undergoing the surgery, there would be nothing that would have kept me away.

The last thing I remembered was counting back from 100. I might have made it to 98.

I was told that there were no unforeseen hiccups with my surgery.

For the next two weeks, I had chest X-rays, scheduled laps around the hospital wing to get my blood flowing and multiple temperature readings. These happened during the day and during the night. I wasn't sleeping well anyway.

Every day since the operation, I had to have my drainage fluid levels measured. It was finally time to get the chest tubes out.

You know you are hungry when hospital food tastes good. After two solid weeks I was finally able to go home. I can't even express how glad I was that I listened to Jean and decided to include Claire in my battle. Doing this alone was something I couldn't fathom.

It felt terrible to think about being a burden to someone, but equally nice that I had someone to lean on.

The doctors were happy with the speed of my recovery. We had to hire a home health-care aide to assist us. Although Claire's devotion was unwavering, it was hard for me to move and I needed assistance with even the smallest walks to the bathroom.

I had lost a considerable amount of weight.

I read the discharge report and it said, "Tight adrenalectomy: diaphragm resection, resection of caudate lobe of the liver, right nephrectomy; partial psoas resection: open cholecystectomy: suture repair of the vena cava and removal of the sarcoma."

No wonder I couldn't walk.

The tumor ended up weighing 20 pounds and was close to 24 inches wide.

Claire

I couldn't believe that this was really happening to us. Poor Gary. When he had gotten the original diagnosis, I really thought if we were diligent with the screenings, we wouldn't have had to face what we just lived through.

I was so scared to lose him. We certainly had been through our share of ups and downs, but we were a team. At the end of the day, there was no doubt that he was my person.

I'm not going to lie. There were times during his treatment that I wanted the pain to go away. Now I craved alcohol, not Adderall. I just longed to escape my thoughts. I didn't do it, though. We had come too far for me to go down that slippery slope.

Drew was coming home a lot. He had offered to move home, but I wanted him to stay at the dorm. I'm sure it was hard for him to put this out of his mind, but I encouraged him to try. He had started dating a new girl named Stacey, but I hadn't met her yet and he said it wasn't serious.

When we were all together, we did a lot of sitting and talking. One of the things that came up was the chance of recurrence.

The doctor told us that after treatment of a primary soft tissue sarcoma, 11 percent to 14 percent of patients developed local recurrence and 18 percent to 50 percent of patients developed metastases.

It was a scary thought, and after watching what Jean went through one that seemed probable. Also, knowing that four of Gary's half-sisters passed of cancer didn't provide any comfort.

After our visit with Bill and Loretta, one thing was very clear. It was important to make the most of the time we had on this earth. The discussions we were having were deep and meaningful. I felt as if we were one person.

We reminisced a lot. Gary had come through the surgery miraculously, but it was hard not to dwell on what came next.

Drew went back to school and when we woke up the next morning, I suggested to Gary that I take a leave of absence and when he was feeling strong enough, we spend some time doing the things we used to love doing.

I referenced Bill's story about how he and Loretta had spent the last couple of months appreciating each other.

I told him I didn't want to spend whatever time we had left in meetings and crunching numbers. Did he?

We had almost lost each other, and we had gotten our second chance.

And then I told him what was truly in my heart: I'd always been an optimist and tried to believe in miracles, but realistically our time together was going to be cut short and I wanted to soak in every minute with him that I could.

Gary

I am so angry that this was happening. Why me? I was feeling fine, but if what the doctor said was true, I had one to three years, three being a stretch.

I wanted to live. I didn't want to leave this earth and I was so scared. I felt like I had wasted my time, spending countless hours at work, being angry, being lazy, being bored. Every minute was a gift I took for granted. Knowing that I wasn't going to see my boy get married and would miss out on a good chunk of life made me so sad. I decided to take Claire up on her proposition to step away from responsibility, not completely, but to make sure that every day meant something.

I planned on still drinking my smoothies and eating all of the cruciferous veggies I could stomach, but now if I felt like having a piece of bacon on a Sunday morning, I wasn't going to deny myself. I was going to savor the flavors.

Each day moving felt a bit better, but I was weak. The surgery had taken a lot out of me. When I tried to create a bucket list in my mind, it wasn't filled with travels or skydiving, but more nights laughing with Claire and Drew. I longed to hold Claire's hand as we went to a concert in the city or perhaps a play.

Things we used to do without thinking twice.

Back then my biggest worry was parking and how far I had to walk from the garage to the theater. I complained about the price of the garage. Now those details seemed so meaningless.

Although I used to love our hikes, I didn't have the stamina I used to, but I still liked to walk, so if the weather permitted, we went to the Cutting Arboretum almost weekly.

Claire still went to Reclaim You, but the focus now was on coping with what may come next with me. She was no longer jittery or trying to do everything. She seemed legitimately contented no matter what we did as long as it was together.

I tried not to beat myself up thinking about the days, months and years we may have wasted.

There were times where we just didn't connect, but when I consider the things that I adored about her, she was definitely the ying to my yang.

Although I didn't want to be obligated to much right now, we did think we should try to find a hobby, for a few reasons. We both were trying not to wait for the next shoe to drop but it was hard not to think about it.

We wanted to do an activity together, and I felt it was important to still socialize.

There wasn't one ounce of me that wanted to try a bowling league, we had already tried cooking, I couldn't really do anything strenuous like pickleball, and golf was just too long of a commitment.

We decided to take a painting class down at the local art league.

There were about 20 people in the class, and the teacher was a man in his mid-60s who had had a successful career as an artist and just did this in his free time.

He played classical music and served wine if you wanted to indulge. Claire and I abstained for obvious reasons, and we learned how to paint.

It was cathartic, fun and for hours a week all I did was concentrate on painting a bowl of fruit.

In my old life BC (before cancer) I never would have taken the time to paint. I loved it, and the fact that we were doing it together made it even more special.

I was a lousy painter, but these canvases would surely end up in the garage anyway.

As the days went on, my strength was coming back. We took a lot of walks now and I decided I was going to ask Claire if we could get a dog. After all, the time away from the house was no longer an issue, and I thought it could be really therapeutic.

Claire

I loved to paint. Who knew? I looked forward to our weekly class and found it so relaxing. It was amazing how much your mind and thinking control your happiness. I was making a real effort to stay in the moment and not anticipate or ruminate. Not an easy task.

Gary just used his sickness card to get us a dog. Well played.

There was a tiny part of me that had always considered getting one, but the responsibility, the mess and the smell always prevented me from giving my blessing.

However, given our new circumstances, I think the unconditional love and companionship would prove good for both of us. I conceded. I guess keeping a pristine house had lost its importance. Don't get me wrong, I was going to try to train the dog to stay off of the furniture and I would lose my mind if he ever chewed up one of my designer bags, but I had lightened up a little, and thought this would bring some joy into the house.

I told Gary to get dressed and meet me at the car. I proceeded to put a blindfold on him. He didn't seem pleased but played along. I told him to chill and drove us to the local animal shelter.

Twenty minutes later I grabbed his hand and led him into puppy heaven. I had decided we should go for a rescue rather than the breeder route.

As soon as we walked in, I saw a smile form on Gary's face. The smell gave it away. I told him he could take the blindfold off and look around to see if we could find our dog.

We were there for hours trying to find our guy. We ended up gravitating to the same Irish terrier.

We learned that obviously from Ireland, the Irish terrier is one of the oldest terrier breeds. They tend to be "respectful, lively, intelligent, protective, dominant and trainable."

Those were some appealing adjectives.

They were hypoallergenic and had a life expectancy of 13 to 15 years. Of course, hearing that brought us back to reality. Did we only have three years?

I shut down that thought.

Our dog would grow to be 24 to 26 pounds. The only thing left to do now was name him.

He immediately warmed up to both of us, licking and gently jumping up for a pat on the head.

We tossed around a bunch of names, Daredevil, Pickles, I liked Bart, but at the end of the day I let Gary choose and our puppy's name was going to be Charlie.

Charlie fit in from the minute he hopped in our car.

He was a love. So affectionate, and it was nice having a little action in the house. He was busy, all right. I did insist on a crate just until we could get him potty trained.

I didn't know the first step about training a dog, so I did what every human does, I YouTubed it.

We had to set up a consistent schedule including when we fed Charlie and walked him. We were very into walking him and spending time outside.

What I learned was that dogs are very clean creatures and didn't like a urine-soaked rug in their living space just as much as we didn't. I could tell this was going to work out.

The crate I selected was big enough that he could lie down, stand up and turn around. The video said that when he felt an urge he would whine and scratch. So, Gary and I sort of sat there waiting for a sign, and as soon as we heard one whimper, we opened the cage, leashed him up and went outside. I had treats in my pocket as a reward.

I had bought wee-wee pads, but the video said that was giving the dog mixed messages about it being OK to pee in his crate, and I certainly didn't want to encourage that.

Dogs could control their bladders for the number of hours corresponding to their age in months up to about nine months to a year. Our little guy was two months old so we figured we would walk him every two hours.

The schedule was first thing in the morning, last thing at night, after playing indoors, after time in the crate, after his nap, after chewing on his toy and after eating.

We were walking him 12 times a day.

What I noticed, though, was I hadn't thought about Gary's cancer since we had brought Charlie home. I don't think Gary did either.

As weeks went on, we didn't have to walk Charlie every two hours and also figured out his diet and feeding schedule.

It was truly like having a baby again, but we both loved it and him.

Charlie was a quick study and loved his treats and us.

Drew, of course, fell in love with Charlie too and was finding a bunch of excuses like laundry and seeing us to stop home and visit.

I was glad that he was still staying at the dorm because we were really close, and I wanted to make sure he found his independence. Don't get me wrong, I loved it when he was around, but between the threat of his dad having a recurrence and my past indiscretions it is almost as if he was the adult checking in on us, and he was too young to carry that burden.

Gary was getting stronger every day. We were able to bike ride and take Charlie on longer walks. I asked Jeff if I could morph my job into a consulting gig to give me the flexibility to still have some income yet spend time with Gary.

We had two follow-ups since the surgery and the scans remained clear.

I had no idea what was ahead, but I was choosing to live for each day and each other. I was so grateful that I was able to learn from my bad choices and from Bill,

Jean and Loretta the importance of living in the moment and stopping to smell the roses.

I would never take Gary for granted again and would continue to celebrate every day we had together.

Gary

Charlie was the best friend and confidante a guy could have. I still loved every FaceTime I had with Henri, but this little buddy was always available and always around when I needed a snuggle.

I was feeling really good, and although I wasn't naïve, I had had two clean scans and was feeling almost back to my old self.

Sometimes when I was feeling sorry for myself, I reflected and remembered that no one really knew how long they had on this earth.

At the rate I was going, I could have continued working 60 hours a week, picking on Claire, playing video games and wasting my life away.

Now I looked at each day as an opportunity. I loved spending time with Claire and Charlie. I loved nature and painting. I visited Drew and spoke to him regularly and I was present.

Now I put my phone down and leave it. No longer am I constantly checking my text messages and what deadlines I needed to adhere to.

I savored my meals and focused on the taste of delicious food that I used to scarf down in between meetings.

I paid attention to how I was feeling and tried to share these feelings with Claire.

I still looked at her in awe. As always, she had risen to the occasion, and I knew she would be by my side no matter how this journey concluded.

Dorothy had it right: "There is no place like home."

ACKNOWLEDGEMENTS

There are many people I would like to thank that helped me to write this novel. First and foremost, my husband Keith Condon, who discovered his biological family through Ancestry.com and life was never the same.

Although the names have been changed, some of this story is very similar to his history. Thankfully, he does not have the Li-Fraumeni Syndrome gene, but Joan, his beloved half-sister, did have the gene and that is what inspired this story.

I would like to thank Joan's husband, Robert Russell, her sister, Margaret Simpson, and her brother, Daniel Muller Ferguson, for their contributions that helped me get the story of Joan "Jean" correct. She was so loved and full of life. She fought hard against this terrible disease. Although taken too soon, she lived her life to the fullest and left a tremendous mark.

She is missed terribly.

Daniel Muller Ferguson wrote the poem that Henri recited. He speaks fluent French, so the version in the book has been translated. He has a book of poetry coming out on Amazon, and this will be included.

As always, I would like to thank Laurie Jackel for her endless patience and input. She read every line as it was being written and made wonderful suggestions.

I would like to also thank my sister, Wendy Valentino, Celeste Beetge and Diana Emmi who also critiqued the story as it was unfolding.

A special thanks to Jen Ferguson, who shared her amazing story with me and inspired the voice of Claire.

I must also thank my editors Laurie Chittenden and Jane O'Brien who fine-tuned the novel.

A special shout-out to my son, Luke Condon, who makes me so proud and inspired every day.

I had never heard of Li-Fraumeni Syndrome prior to my husband finding his biological father, but it is a horrible genetic mutation that has no cure.

I am hoping this brings some attention to the disease, and also that we remember how precious life and family truly are.

ABOUT THE AUTHOR

Laurie Condon has been writing articles and blogs for two decades. Most of them focus on Fitness, and self-care. They have appeared in Ms. Fitness, Personal Fitness Professional, Health Products Business, Club Industry, The Nutritious Life Studio and S-Life Magazine. Her first book with Black Rose Writing is *Everything Is A Big Deal, Until It's Not*. She self-published a book entitled *Keeping Fit on The Run*, which was purchased by a company for their salespeople. She lives on Long Island with her husband and their son.

NOTE FROM THE AUTHOR

Word-of-mouth is crucial for any author to succeed. If you enjoyed *There's No Place Like Home*, please leave a review online—anywhere you are able. Even if it's just a sentence or two. It would make all the difference and would be very much appreciated.

Thanks!
Laurie Condon

We hope you enjoyed reading this title from:

BLACK ROSE
writing™

www.blackrosewriting.com

Subscribe to our mailing list – *The Rosevine* – and receive **FREE** books, daily deals, and stay current with news about upcoming releases and our hottest authors.
Scan the QR code below to sign up.

Already a subscriber? Please accept a sincere thank you for being a fan of Black Rose Writing authors.

View other Black Rose Writing titles at www.blackrosewriting.com/books and use promo code
PRINT to receive a **20% discount** when purchasing.